Handsome ...

Each component of the Austin A40 chassis is fashioned from highest grade materials, engineered to precise limits and assembled by the automobile industry's most advanced techniques. Most notable among these components are the high-efficiency engine, four-speed synchromesh transmission, spiral bevel rear axle, independent coil-spring front suspension, hydraulic brakes and cam gear steering. The frame itself, individually constructed of box-section steel, offers robust support being an integral unit entirely separate from the body. It forms the basis of a car that is sturdily built for lively performance and dependable service. Left-hand steering is fitted.

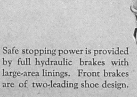
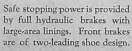

Safe stopping power is provided by full hydraulic brakes with large-area linings. Front brakes are of two-leading shoe design.

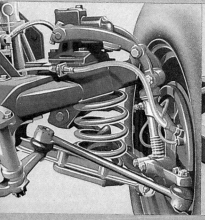

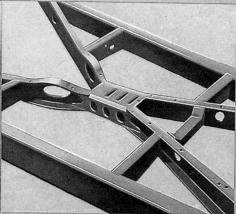

To take the rough with the smooth and afford even riding on highways or tracks—the A40 independent coil-spring front suspension.

Sturdy-cross bracing is incorporated in the individual box-section steel chassis frame to give long-lasting strength and dependability.

MOTORTHERAPY & OTHER STORIES

BILL SCHERMBRUCKER

TALONBOOKS   VANCOUVER   1993

Published with the assistance of the Canada Council

Talonbooks
201-1019 East Cordova
Vancouver, British Columbia
Canada V6A 1M8

This book was typesct in Garamond and Avant Garde by Pièce de Résistance Ltée., and printed by Hignell Printing Ltd.

First Printing: August 1993

Acknowledgments:

Versions of some of these stories have appeared in *Canadian Fiction Magazine, Grain, Prison Journal* and *The Capilano Review*, and on CBC Radio. "Like a Hinge on a Gate" was given an honourable mention in John Updike's annual *Best American Short Stories*. Thanks to Jean Clifford, Penny Connell, Graham Forst, Sharon Schermbrucker, Audrey Thomas and Karl Siegler for continuing editorial advice.

The cover pictures are from an original Austin A-40 sales brochure, published by the Austin Motor Company of England, and provided by Packard enthusiast Richard C.W. Percy of Coquitlam, courtesy Archibald Rollo, Column One Editor, *The Vancouver Sun.*

Canadian Cataloguing in Publication Data
 Schermbrucker, William Gerald, 1938—
 Motortherapy & other stories

  ISBN 0-88922-330-0

  I. Title.
  PS8587.C435M6 1993   C813'.54   C93-091703-0
  PR9199.3.S266M6 1993

Contents

For Dave Brewster,
wherever you are now

WRITTEN IN CARS
A PREFACE

Young men riding in the street
In the bright new season
Spur without reason
Causing their steeds to leap

— *Ezra Pound, "Image from D'Orleans"*

My parents' last resort, to get me to sleep on bad nights, was to put me in the car and drive around for a while. They'd try gripe water, changing me again, patting my back till I burped . . . still I'd be screaming my head off. Eventually my father would grab the key, toss me in the back of the Morris 10, turn on and press the starter button, and bingo, I'd shut up. Then he'd drive till I fell asleep, and he'd carry me back inside.

It seems to be a universal therapy, driving. My friend Peggy told me that in California, when life got too stressful or boring, she used to go out on the freeway in the middle of the night, and drive for hours to Berkeley, and back again. Over a period of months she began to recognize some of the cars, and she figured there were other people out there doing the same thing. Anyway, it worked for me as an infant, and I remember it working again about thirty years later. It was in upstate New York, on a night when I was miserable after a break-up, and I got into a van with some friends after dinner, and we drove to Buffalo to see *Deliverance*. Lying in the back of the van, taking an unaccustomed puff on a joint someone passed me, my head against the back door as we whizzed down the New York State Thruway, I suddenly felt more peaceful than I had in many years.

I looked at the outline of the shoulders up ahead, and found myself wanting to switch the two silhouettes around. They were sitting on the passenger bench, the man on the left and the woman on the right. Why was I trying to reverse them? Suddenly I realized I had slipped right back to Africa, and that was my Mum and Dad up there, only my Dad would normally have been on the right, driving. I pushed the top of my head comfortably against the back door, and thought, "Well, if we get rear-ended, so be it." I was sleeping peacefully long before we arrived at the movie.

My memory of being driven around the block in the Morris 10 was reinforced by the dozens of times my father told the story at dinner. He would also tell about my brother and me going out to the back of my great-uncle's house in Eldoret and driving cars. When a car died, Uncle Doc would put it out in the back "to use for parts." That's what he said, but I don't know if it was true, since they were all different makes; I think he may have just been nostalgic about parting with them. At any rate, there were five or six derelict cars lined up on blocks beside the old tennis court with a corrugated iron roof over them. Whenever another one died, the roof was simply extended. So my brother and I would spend all day out there in the Hudson, the Essex, the Packard or the Chev, swirling the wheel through lean-out hairpin bends, stretching our feet for the pedals, squeezing the gear lever lock to shift down for a hill. Sometimes we raced one another, and sometimes we teamed up and drove the same car, him at the wheel, me on the gears. He did the engine with a loud, rising hum, and it was really satisfying to me to change the gear, and hear the pitch go low again. Breakdowns were no problem. If it was a puncture, one of us would get out and kick at the blocks where the wheels should have been. If it was mechanical, my brother would get out with a tire lever or a starting handle, and I'd hold up one hinged side of the hood while he took a swing at the engine. Years later, when I revisited Eldoret, I went behind the house to see the cars, and noticed that the spark plugs and distributor caps were all smashed to pieces.

My friend Marcel said the other day: "The self-expressive imagination finds objects in the physical surroundings to make into personal metaphors." Of course it does! My whole life is written in cars, and so is his I should think. Maybe everyone's is: those who have them, and those who don't; those who trade them in before the warranty expires, those who never buy a new one; those who can't operate the seat belts, and mistrust their mechanics, and those who are forever getting grease on their hands and leaving it on the steering wheel. Marcel drove up beside me in his gleaming new Infiniti with keyless entry and all-electric mirrors. He shook his head sadly at the dust and the rust on my old station wagon which my son has christened "The Ambulance." "When are you going to get yourself something decent to drive?" said Marcel. "Just *look* at this mess."

"Okay," I said, "look *at* it. And now look at yours. Which one would you say more accurately reflects our spiritual condition?"

THE RIGHT TOOLS

"Always carry a bar of soap," my father said. It wasn't clear to me how you could fix a leak in the gas tank with soap. But I never doubted that sort of instruction, coming from him. I was nineteen then, with a B.A., and had started teaching at the Delamere High School, Nairobi. I'd been writing letters to a girl in Johannesburg named Julia, whom I knew from University, and before the school holidays I bumped into a friend who told me he and some other guys were going to drive a Land Rover to London, through the Sahara Desert. "Damn it," I thought, "*I* am going to drive to Johannesburg!"

The Easter school holiday was only three weeks, and to go out of the country you needed permission from the Principal.

"Jo-*hannes*-burg!" Mr. McGowan knit his grave brows. "Tanganyika, through Northern Rhodesia, Southern Rhodesia, the length of the Transvaal. Then *back* again! Would there be time for all of that?"

1

"Sir, I give you my word I'll be here for the first day of term."

My father was horrified. "In that old Austin!" He stood chewing the inside of his cheek. Then, with the whine of a man losing control of his children, he said: "At *least* go and get yourself a travel mate. I'd hate to think of you alone on that road." He had driven it himself after the War, and knew the difficulties. I went to the Royal East African Automobile Association office on Delamere Avenue. The clerk flipped through some cards and found a 40-year-old British bricklayer, Len, wanting a ride to Salisbury, to look for work. I didn't tell my father that. He thought my mate was in it for the round trip.

"Got all the tools you need?"

I had a couple of tire levers, two open-ended wrenches, a small file, a pair of pliers and a screwdriver.

"I've got everything, Father," I said. "Even the bar of soap."

"Well good luck, my boy. At least you have a full moon to help you."

We set off the next morning. Len drove on the dirt road from Kajiado to Namanga, and his slow braking made me resolve he would never drive my car again.

It began with the hubcaps. I had decided to leave them at home, to avoid their being stolen. I thought hubcaps were decoration. Approaching a bridge on a very rough road, I was trying to accelerate to 40, to ride the corrugations, and the car was shaking dreadfully. Suddenly there was a violent lurch. I braked and we hit the ground on the left.

Broken spring? I wondered.

To my surprise, a wheel went bouncing down the road and flew up over the edge of the bridge.

I leaped from the car and ran. The wheel was floating in the brown water of the river. I dashed down through

2

tearing thorns and tall green grass, and got to it half a mile downstream, where it had washed into the reeds. In the hot, animal-smelling stillness I stood, bleeding and muddy, and caught my breath. We searched in the dust along the edges of the road, but could find not one of the wheel nuts. I took a nut off each of the other three wheels.

"Let's 'ope there's no more problems, then!" said Len cheerfully, and lit a cigarette.

We slept in the car outside the station at Dodoma, and drove on at first light. After Iringa, the road crossed mountain ridges with rivers between. Instead of bridges there were concrete drifts, and at each drift we got out and walked through, probing with a stick. When the water was too high, I took off the fan belt lest we stall in midstream from wet plugs. After the last drift, we were singing George Formby songs, and crossed a small bridge, not noticing a big rock on the other side. The Austin bounced up on its old coil springs, I caught a glimpse of the rock, braked, and the car came crashing down.

"Argh! The tie rod!" I cried.

But it was worse. There was a terrific bang, and a loud staccato knocking came from the engine. I switched it off at once.

"We can't have run the bearings just like that!" I said.

I looked under the front of the car and saw a dent in the oilpan, so huge, I realized the bearing caps must have been hitting it on the inside. A line of dark oil was trickling out.

"Not so bad," I said. "Just a buggered sump."

"Wha' yer gunner do then?" asked Len.

"Ee, I'm gunner fix it, that's wha'."

We pushed the car to a sandy spot beneath a baobab tree and scooped out a trench under the engine. It was a hot, stuffy morning, but the baobab gave cool shade. Flies crawled on my face, and I banged my head on metal shaking them off. Hot oil dripped onto the only shirt I had brought. I worked and whistled.

"'Ow yer gunner fix it, Alistair?"

"Take it off and go get it beaten out and welded."

"Weldid! There's no friggin' weldin' shop 'ere. Is there?"

I didn't answer. Was it sixty-five miles to Tunduma, or was it ninety?

Len suddenly scrambled to his feet, kicking sand in my eye.

"Yikes man!" he cried. "There's *neh*-tives 'ere!"

I crawled out, wiped my face on my sleeve, and saw three small children staring wide-eyed from the bushes.

"Jambo," I said, but they just blinked.

"Scary, hey Len?" I laughed.

"No, *look ere*," he said vehemently, "where there's kids there's a whole friggin' village. 'Appen we just *drive on!* Fix it later."

"Len," I said, "that rock was just the beginning. Down the road they've got a ditch dug. Cannibal food trap, man!"

Len got in the car, and locked the door.

"Hey, I can't get underneath with your weight sitting in it!"

He wouldn't move, so I had to scrape the trench deeper. I took off a dozen setscrews holding the oilpan, but the back three were in a narrow cleft between the rear wall of the pan and the clutch housing. I could get the wrench positioned on the head of a screw with the tip of my finger in the other end, but there was no way to apply force.

"Right tools for the job!" I said out loud, remembering Roger Worthington, my flat-mate at the University of Cape Town. He had a Citroen Light Fifteen, and had taught me most of what I knew about cars. He was a very careful mechanic. Once our other flat-mate Andy showed us a wrench he had bent open trying to tighten cylinder-head nuts, and Roger just shook his head. "You should have used a ring spanner or a socket wrench," he said in disgust. When Andy had gone, he told me in a deep, serious voice: "It's really important, Alistair, to have the right tools for the job. Never forget that."

4

I remembered it now, and felt a pang of defeat. I searched the car, stared into the trunk, into the engine. I emptied the glove compartment. Nothing. The three children followed, watching, as I walked over to the bush, put my hands on my hips, and stared dumbly ahead. There in front of me was a bit of half-inch pipe sticking out of a lump of concrete. I thought, "Well, if the Mau-Mau could produce home-made guns out of iron piping, surely I can file it into a tubular wrench. *Tubular wrench!*" I ran back to the car.

Under the battery, some previous owner had welded in a support bracket, using a tubular wrench as one of the stays. I broke it out with pliers, cleaned up one end with the file, and hammered it with the tire lever to make it fit the retaining screws.

Giddy from heat and hunger, I crawled under and tried it. Too short to clear the oilpan housing. I needed an extension, an L-shaped key. I filed and bent a bolt I took off the back bumper. A piece of iron piping gave me leverage, and the screws turned easily.

I got the oilpan off, and sure enough there were bright marks in the soft iron, where the bearing caps had banged into it. To be certain, I started the engine and ran it for a second. No knock! So, no run bearings . . . it was just the damaged oilpan I had to fix.

I picked up the oilpan and began to walk down the road. Len rolled down his window and shouted: "Alistair, if you find a shop, buy some fags. Matinees if possible."

The early afternoon sun was brutal. I walked on the dry, red sand, and saw rings in front of my eyes. A pickup truck was coming, and I lifted my hand. The driver, an African trader, told me there was a big garage, *"kubwa sana,"* a couple of miles down the road, with welding equipment. The two women sitting in the back, one with a baby at her breast, gave me big smiles and waves as they drove off.

For two solid hours I walked in a trance, unaware of my surroundings till I came upon a road gang.

"Where you take this?" demanded the PWD foreman, in his khaki uniform with green pointing.

"My *gari* hit a rock," I said. "I am taking the sump to the garage." I pointed hopefully into the near distance. "They can *choma* it here, I'm told."

He shook his head.

"Somebody joke you," he said. No garage till Mbeya. Seventah-two miles." Swinging to point in the other direction down the road, he added, "Or Iringa, sickisty-seven miles."

"You *sure?* No welding round here?"

"*Haki, bwana!* Nothing."

"Bloody hell! Why would the guy tell me?"

The foreman dropped his eyes. "Some of these fellows are crazy," he said morosely. Near Dodoma, some children had taunted us with the two-finger sign for freedom and shouted *"Uhuru!"* as we passed, but I couldn't believe the trickery of that pickup driver.

When I got back to the car, I could smell cooking fires.

"Wha' yer gunner do now?"

I went down to the stream, but leaped back promptly when a vicious-eyed yellow snake sprang out at me, then slithered away. I chose a smooth stone and beat out the dent, then turned the oilpan over and tapped the lips of torn metal together. I poured some oil in, and it ran straight through. I took the screwdriver and the stone and banged away to seal the lips. Roger Worthington, my father . . . I had to smile thinking of them now.

I tore a piece of rag, and jammed it with a screwdriver from inside the oilpan into the lips of the tear. I bit off a corner of the bar of soap, and chewed it till it was soft, and smeared it into the tear, inside and out, plastering the outside with a paste of soap, grease and sand, hoping it would set. I replaced the oilpan on the car, and poured a pint of oil in, and got under to watch. The light was fading. No leak, not a single drop. Problem solved. I drove on south in absolute confidence.

Near Tunduma, the car slowed down of its own accord, and came to a stop on a small hill. Both front brake drums burned my finger when I touched them. I crawled under, and managed to turn a bleed nipple with the pliers, and relieved the pressure. But the brakes bound up again as soon as I hit the pedal. I bled them again, and drove slowly, without braking. At Tunduma, the mechanic at the service station said: "I can fix that, no problem. Master cylinder kit. Leave the car with me overnight." He directed us to an old wood-and-iron hotel, a relic from the German days.

Next day we crossed into Northern Rhodesia, and I noticed the steering was becoming heavy. Then the brakes bound again. I stopped and checked the tire pressures, and bled off some fluid, and we reverted to driving using only the gears for braking. So much for the master cylinder overhaul!

All of a sudden, near Kapiri Mposhi, I saw a ploughshare sign to Sir James MacIntyre's farm and swung off. Elspeth, his daughter, had been Julia's flat-mate at university, and took over from me the night-school we ran for blacks. At the house, Elspeth greeted us with her Cupid's bow lips and bright, intelligent eyes. An older man in work clothes, Elspeth's uncle, walked around the Austin with a puzzled expression.

"Pull in over the pit, son. Let me take a look."

In the pit, he shone a light.

"I thought the car was standing odd. See? Front cross member of your chassis is cracked." He moved the light. "Both sides."

True enough, there were jagged quarter-inch cracks at the junctures of the steel frame. I couldn't believe it. My car!

"I noticed the steering's heavy," I said.

"Of course. Your front wheels are splayed out. Look! Tires just about worn through."

"What on earth can I do?"

"Nothing here. Chassis'll have to be bent back in a

hydraulic press. And arc welded. He clenched his fists, and drew his elbows together, miming the way the press would bend the metal straight again for welding. "If worst comes to worst," he said gloomily, "you might need this *riem.*" He handed me a rawhide thong, about twenty feet long. I had a vision of my car being towed by oxen.

"Stay to dinner," said Elspeth, and we gladly accepted. But then guests began arriving in formal attire.

"Once a month we have Scottish country dancing," Elspeth said.

"And here *we* are! A couple of fools in dirty khaki shorts!"

"Nonsense," said Sir James. "You're on the road. Everybody understands."

After dinner, the ladies retired into the house, and Sir James led the men discreetly out to the lawn. The moon was not yet up, but each of us found a convenient spot to unbutton—except Len, who suddenly called aloud:

"What are we all standing out here for?"

We said goodbye to the MacIntyres and I was thankful to drive away. The brakes were clear, but now the engine was running rough. Nightjars roosted in the road, and flew up as the car lights woke them. After the second sickening thud, I couldn't stand any more death, and pulled off under a big tree. We slept till dawn.

The road from Lusaka to Salisbury wound through hills of scraggly thorn brush. We drove on two blacktop strips, and whenever another car approached, we had to get off one strip and back up again. Half an hour of that and the right front tire blew. I put on the spare. Then the left one blew.

"Drive on the rim," said Len. "It's too dangerous to stop here."

"Oh, shut up, would you!"

Anxiously, I jacked the car, levered the broken casing off the rim and stuffed in twigs, leaves, hessian, and the rawhide, as a cushion. We crawled on, with the engine running very rough and the sound of the crumpled tire hard to bear. I was relieved when we reached a flat area, and could pull off the road.

"I'll have to hitch-hike and buy a new tire," I said.

Len pointed to a red-lettered notice board:

"TSETSE CONTROL AREA
KEEP WINDOWS ROLLED UP
DRIVE AT 30 M.P.H. MINIMUM"

The first vehicle to stop was a refrigerator truck, with a black driver.

"I'm not riding with 'im," said Len.

I climbed aboard, and that was the last I ever saw of Len. The truck driver said there was a welder up ahead at Sinoia who could fix anything. "Two pound, three pound, he charge you four and sixpence an inch."

I had fifteen pounds to get me to Johannesburg. The new tire would take half of that.

"No good leave your car till night," the driver said. "Thieves!" he grinned. "Battery, tires, *nothing* will remain." He let me off at a service station showing a Goodyear sign, and I got a new tire, and hitched back in a silver Standard Vanguard, and reached the Austin around four p.m. Alone, my car disabled under the tsetse fly warning sign, I found it impossible to stretch the new tire onto the rim with the short tire levers. I thought of those rotating pneumatic machines they had in service stations, and wanted to cry.

I opened the gold-edged pages of my New Testament at random, and read aloud:

"And the rain descended, and the floods came, and the winds blew, and beat upon that house; and it fell: and great was the fall of it."

I shut the little blue leather book. Tears rolled down my face.

Then I got angry, thinking of Len. If it hadn't been for his need to get to Salisbury, instead of turning left after Lusaka, I'd have turned right, and gone straight down to Bulawayo. My uncle's farm was there, on the Umgusa

Irrigation. I seized the tire levers again, and this time, miraculously, the new tire went onto the rim. By five o'clock I was moving once more, though the car stank of burnt brake linings.

At Sinoia, I found the Blue Star Welding yard. Nobody was there. It was Easter Monday. I drove into the yard, put the car up on blocks, and removed all the steering gear I could get off the chassis. Money or no money, I was not sleeping in the car, I decided. I walked to the hotel, and took a shared room for the night, for sixteen shillings. I ate supper, and carried a Castle Lager out to the wooden verandah. A guy asked if he could join me, and I told him my story. He knew the Blue Star welder, and described how to get to his house.

"Take my car," he said, and tossed me the keys.

The welder was finishing his meal, but offered to come and do the job at once.

"The morning will be fine," I said. "I just wanted to alert you to the fact that my car's in your yard."

My room-mate in the hotel, a huge fellow my own age, told me he was working on the construction of the Kariba dam.

"It's such a drag," he said. "Every weekend, to see my girlfriend in Salisbury, I have to drive *seventy miles!*"

I laughed, and didn't tell him what I was doing.

There was a pay-phone in the hotel. The operator told me a call to Johannesburg would cost six shillings for three minutes. I phoned and got Julia's sister.

"Where are you?" she asked.

"Sinoia."

"Julia, Julia!" I heard Sarah shouting. "Alistair's in Pretoria."

Julia came on and said, "Shall we heat you up some supper?"

"I'm in *Sinoia*," I enunciated. "The other side of Salisbury. Seven hundred miles from you."

Next morning, when I got to the welding yard, the job

was finished. He had left the steering parts for me to put back. He charged me ten shillings, and wouldn't take more. For another thirty shillings, the service station overhauled my brake master cylinder. I drove out of Sinoia feeling terrific. With its light steering, the A40 handled like a brand new car, though the engine jerked and stuttered. I braked, and braked again, and whistled with joy.

It began to rain, and I was on a curve, when the car lurched left in a way that was now familiar. I was coming up to a concrete bridge, so I steered off the road and aimed for smaller thorn bushes. The car bounced around and finally stopped. I took my clothes off, got out, and searched in my underwear till I found the missing wheel.

A car stopped on the road.

"Could you stop at the Sinoia Garage, and tell that idiot he stripped my nuts when he put the wheel back on? The A40 from Kenya, he'll remember."

An hour later, the young mechanic arrived in a pickup.

"I'm *terribly* sorry," he said. "I've got a good used hub here." He held it up.

"Man, that's got five studs. That's for an A70 or an A90."

"Now I feel really stupid!" he said. He kneeled down in the grass and examined my hub.

"You know what, though?" he said. "These are longer nuts. And your threads are good on the ends. I bet they'll hold."

He was right. He refused payment, and wished me a good trip, and said sorry again. It was only as I drove away that I realized the hub with the stripped threads was on the left, and it was the right one he had taken off to check the binding brakes. I was filled with guilt, as I drove on to Salisbury.

I found Roger Worthington's room in the student residence, and climbed through the window and fell asleep on his bed. When he arrived, he told me he was taking an Education degree. We decided to drive through the night to Bulawayo, and he would hitch-hike back the next day. I told him about getting my oilpan off, and I showed him the tool I had made. He turned the tubular wrench and key in his fingers, with a smile. "Right tools," he said.

Driving at three a.m., I was jabbering away when Roger suddenly cried "Stop!" and I stood on the brakes. The car came to a halt about an arm's length from a goods train that was rocketing through the level crossing.

We looked at one another, and Roger shook his head.

At dawn, he asked, "But why's your engine so rough?"

I pulled off the road, and we took a look under the hood.

"'Struth, man!" said Roger. "Carburettor's cracked right off at the mount. Must be that heavy air cleaner. Why do they make carburettors out of shit metal? African roads kill them."

In Bulawayo, he directed me to a wrecking yard where we found a used carburettor. I said goodbye to Roger, then it was nonstop to Johannesburg. I had four days, but I was so busy working on the car, I barely had time to relate to Julia. We went to the movies one night, and saw Pat Boone in *April Love*.

One morning, her father asked me to give him a ride in to his city law firm. By Zoo Lake Park, he said:

"Alistair, if it should be the case that you've come down here to ask us if we think you would make a suitable son-in-law, then I must tell you that the answer to that question would be yes."

I was dumbfounded.

I had eight days to get home, and it took me nine. I sent McGowan a telegram: "BROKEN DOWN STOP REGRET BROKEN TRUST STOP HURRYING." I waited to send it from the Post Office in Broken Hill.

When I got home, McGowan was tickled, and wanted to hear the whole story: the cracked chassis, the valve seat insert that sprang out at Beit Bridge, and how the Bulawayo machine shop opened for me on a Sunday. I told him about the Jehovah's Witness convert with his chicken, hitch-hiking five hundred miles to a convention; about picking up Guddy Hansen on the way home, how we had to wait all night for the river to go down, how we lost both tire chains in a rainstorm, and had to grope about in the deep mud in our underwear to recover them. And Julia, the girl I went to see—I hinted at her. I told everybody these stories. That trip was a real rite of passage for me. It resulted in marriage, children, divorce, and all the rest of it.

But there was one thing I did not tell. I never mentioned to anyone how I fixed my broken oilpan with a piece of cloth and a bar of soap. I simply *forgot*, until today. I had intended to get it welded in Johannesburg, but seeing my muddy green Austin right on the posh city street at Hillbrow, looking so strange with its EA(K) international plate amid all those foreign Transvaal numbers, I felt euphoric and careless. For another year, I drove that Austin merrily around Nairobi, and when the steering box broke I sold it "as is" for fifteen pounds. "Wery durable model," Jamal Habib said. "As long you fix, they last for ever."

Cars don't rust in Nairobi. Some do last forever. Hey, If you're ever in Kenya, keep an eye open for a pale green '49 A40 Devon, with a sliding sun roof. W381. If you see it, kneel down and scratch with your fingernail at the left front edge of the oilpan, would you? If you find soap, let me know.

LIKE A HINGE ON A GATE

"He's not new to Africa," the Old Man said. "He's just done his teaching diploma at Makerere. But he's new to Kenya, and he's new to teaching. Would you be so good as to take him under your wing when he arrives?"

"Yes sir," I said. "I'll be glad to. Where is he from?"

The Old Man's eagle brows contracted, which always made him look like the Cambridge don he would have been if he hadn't opted for the Church Missionary Society, and Africa, thirty years before.

"He's . . . an American," he said reluctantly. "But I've had a talk with him, and he's . . . a *good* American. There are some, you know."

"What do you suppose the Old Man means by that?" I asked Julia when I told her."

"Perhaps he's respectful."

"Perhaps he talks quietly," I suggested.

I was dead wrong. So was Julia. And the Old Man was right, in ways I had yet to learn about.

Jedediah Quimby III was a tall New-Englander, twenty-three, with a wave of sandy hair and a ruddy face. When you told him things, he listened, nodding, with a steady frown. He took matters seriously. I used to think it had something to do with the five divorces his parents had racked up between them. (I remember, years later, when he was running for political office in New Hampshire, listening to him answer a question on a radio interview:

"Mr. Quimby, would you be in favour of impeachment proceedings against President Nixon?"

"I uh—" he began, and sitting out in the lobby of the radio station, I could visualize Jed's frowning face bobbing around in a figure eight as he swung his body in the chair to address the grave issue head-on.

"I believe in the principle of innocent until proven guilty."

"So—"

"So I would have to look at the full evidence before I could answer you."

"Then—"

"BUT . . . based on some of the things I have heard, IF they turn out to be true—"

"You—"

"*I* would impeach."

"You—"

"*I* would impeach."

In all his moral seriousness, Jed Quimby sounded a bit too much like Nixon himself, so the voters of New Hampshire did not choose him.)

No sooner had Jed arrived at the school, than he got into conflict with the Vice-principal. It was at the first staff meeting. The Principal, the Old Man himself, swung his gaze round the room at the end of the meeting, and asked if there was any other business.

"Uh. . . ."

"Yes, Jed?"

"Sir, the urinals . . . the School's urinals. . . ."

"What about them, Jed?"

"They're absolutely disgraceful, sir. They smell very bad."

Vice-principal Arthur Jamieson cleared his throat deliberately. He'd been there over thirty years, from the time when the school consisted of two wooden shacks, and the only toilet facility was a length of two-by-four set over a trench in the wattle forest. Now this Yank, with two weeks under his belt. . . .

"I would not have thought this an ap*prop*riate discussion." Jamieson rolled his R's.

The Old Man considerèd for a moment, then nodded. "Let's close in prayer," he said.

That night, Jed marched back and forth across our living-room rug, his voice growing louder and more rhetorical, till the dog started barking at his heels, and woke the baby.

The following staff meeting, under "any other business," Jed raised his hand, and got the nod.

"I'd like the School's permission to spend three hundred and fifty shillings on maintenance."

It was a fair sum of money, about half a month's pay for a junior teacher.

"On what, Jed?" the Old Man asked. Jamieson's face was grey as a church stone.

"Paint, sir."

"Paint?"

"I have arranged with Shivji Brothers Ltd. to seal the walls of the urinals with waterproof paint. Here's the contract, I just need your permission." He waved a piece of paper in the air.

"It's an in-*or*-dinate sum," Jamieson declared. "There are higher priorities."

"I'm prepared to pay it myself," Jed said. "I just need permission."

The Old Man blinked slowly, twice, and his face cracked half a smile. "Let's close in prayer," he said.

Afterwards, he took the paper from Jed, and the school paid. The smell ended. But the war was on.

Next Staff Meeting:

"I underr-stand, there is a plan a-foot, for *mixed singing!*" Jamieson enunciated the words slowly, as though "mixed singing" was the name of a rare disease.

In the silence that followed, people began slowly to focus on one person.

"Jed?" said the Old Man.

"I uh. . . ." Jed's red face went even redder. His brows knit, and his head bobbed, as he shifted in the chair. "I have been in consultation with Miss Merivale at the girls' school, and with Dr. Taylor at the Conservatory. We are all agreed that a choir drawn from the two schools would be of great value. With a choir of mixed voices, we can greatly expand the repertoire we can perform. At present we are limited by the artificial division. On an experimental basis, we propose rehearsing one evening a week."

"Evenings!" cried Jamieson. But Jed got his way.

The next incident concerned furniture, which brings us to Solomon.

I would not have been surprised if Jed had refused to have a servant. The British expatriate teachers all had servants as a matter of course—why deprive yourself of the convenience, given how cheap they were, and anyway it created employment. But as an American, Jed saw emerging Africa differently. Julia and I had resisted having an inside servant, and we were thought quite modern for this. I would have expected Jed's Yankee egalitarianism to have revolted against the idea of personal service. But he surprised us all.

"This is Solomon," he said, introducing me to a small, very black man who was seated in an armchair in the living room. "This is my friend Alistair."

"How do you do," I said, and reached out a hand. I spoke in English, taking Solomon to be a teaching colleague, or one of Jed's fellow-students from Makerere who'd dropped in for tea.

"I'll get you a cup," said Jed, and made for the kitchen. Solomon let go my grasp and said, "No, Bwana Mkubwa, I get it." He moved swiftly, and beat Jed to the doorway.

"I'm glad you stopped by," Jed said to me. "We're about to discuss wages. Perhaps you could give me your advice."

"Perhaps I could."

Solomon returned with my cup, and poured it full.

"Soogar?"

"Sucari mbili, asante."

"Oh!" Solomon beamed. *"Bwana najua kiswahili msuri sana!"*

"Thank you," I said in Swahili, "and your English is good, too. You're not from round here, are you? What's your tribe, Muluhia?"

"Yes!" His coal-black face positively shone. I had taken a risk guessing about this sensitive subject.

"Listen, Solomon," I said, still in Swahili, "we don't say 'Bwana' around here very much any more."

"Oh yes, Bwana, I understand!"

"What is all this 'bwana' business?" Jed broke in. "What do you call me, 'Bwana' what?"

"You are Bwana Mkubwa, Bwana. It mean you big man." He held his hand above his head to indicate Jed's height, and smiled innocently.

I laughed. No fool, this Solomon. He laughed with me.

"And you," Jed said, looking down seriously on Solomon's head, "you are rather short. So how do you say that in Swahili?"

"Kidogo," said Solomon.

"Bwana Kidogo?" Jed tried.

"With *Bwana* we say *mdogo*."

Jed held out his hand. *"Jambo, Bwana Mdogo!"*

"Jambo Bwana Mkubwa!" said Solomon.

I watched them shake hands, grinning, and I realized that neither of them knew what kind of pact they had sealed with one another—nor, for that matter, did I. Later, I tried to explain to Jed the subtlety of Solomon's humour. In

1961, with Kenya's Independence on the horizon, no black man called any white man "Bwana Mkubwa," except perhaps tongue in cheek. Solomon, having done it, and then embarrassed by my presence, now pretended it referred to height.

"It would be like some man in India addressing you as 'Mighty Sahib'."

"I don't know, man," Jed knit his brows. "I think it's quite literal. The tall gentleman, the short gentleman."

"Oh sure," I said. "Abbott and Costello."

They settled the details: wages, rations, days off. The house had three bedrooms, and Jed suggested Solomon use one of them.

"Oh no, Bwana Mkubwa, not here. This one out here." He pointed to the small servant's house at the back of the lot. "This good for me."

"It's very small," said Jed. There was one room, and a shower stall with a flush hole, and a kitchen recess. "It's too small."

"*I* am too small," said Solomon. "It good for me."

"All right." Jed frowned. "Now, what about furniture? Bed, table, chairs."

Solomon shrugged.

"Why don't you take the furniture out of my spare bedroom?" Jed said.

"Thank you, Bwana."

But when Solomon went next door to borrow a wrench to undo the bolts on the bed, the information fed into the grapevine, and quickly reached the ears of the Vice-principal. Jamieson drove over to Jed's at once, and delivered a stern harangue on "setting bad precedents." He pointed out that the furniture belonged to the school, and that the school could "in no wise countenance" its being loaned to a servant.

An hour later, Jed was tramping back and forth on our living-room floor, re-enacting the harangue, with an accurate imitation of Jamieson's thistly accent. He ended, on the moral zenith of his lungs: "So Solomon, man, is OUT there, SLEEPING ON A COLD CEMENT FLOOR! *TO AVOID SETTING BAD PRECEDENTS!*"

The dog barked, and feinted at Jed's knees. The baby woke. Julia sighed.

Poor Jed.

"Always there is this grey and unimaginative presence, telling me I cannot do the things I want to do. The same at Harvard, man! The same at Makerere!"

Later, I learned that at Harvard he had been forbidden to use props belonging to the dramatic society, for a play he was producing, so he sent his actors and stage hands to steal scenery, from various amateur companies, or wherever they could. This brought the Cambridge police to the opening performance, but the play did go on. And at Makerere University, in Uganda, he had wanted to put on Macbeth in Maasai tribal dress, and had been refused by some university authority who said that such a show would not attract a large enough audience. Jed wired friends and relatives in the States, and raised $500, and rented the national Theatre in Kampala. "And made a *profit* man! *We made a profit!* Two-hundred and eighty shillings."

Jed's relationship with Solomon settled into a routine, but it took a while, and it took some learning on Jed's part. The fact is, he needed a servant, more than some of the other bachelor teachers, who at least cooked for themselves. Jed's mind was usually on a project, the choir, the Drama Festival—even the blessed urinals—and he forgot about the humdrum details of life. Cutlery, for instance, cooking utensils, even an iron. Once the bed problem was solved (I had taken him down to the native market, and he bought a hand-hewn thong bed for ten shillings) Jed simply left the rest to Solomon. And Solomon took care of things, borrowing an iron from us, pots and pans from Mary Greene; sheets, pillow cases, towels, etc. Solomon found them all for Jed, as the need arose. I learned that he had even bought plates in the *boma* with a few shillings of his own money.

It was the coffee pot that clarified the relationship. Jed had met a young teacher at the Girls' School, and after much fretting, had invited her to dinner, followed by a movie in Nairobi. He brought her home at midnight for coffee, but was unable to find the coffee pot. It had been there at dinner, and now damn it, the thing was gone. He pondered all the possibilities, and eliminated them. Then he stood confidently on the back step and yelled into the darkness:

"Bwana Mdogo! Bwana Mdogo!"

At length came the weary answer, "Y-es Bwana."

"You have my coffee pot?"

"Y-es Bwana."

"Well bring it back, right now!"

"I sleeping, Bwana."

"Yes. And I wish to make coffee."

A few minutes later, the pot was pushed through the back door.

"Your coffee pot."

"Damn right. And I would appreciate it in future if you would not borrow my things without asking."

The next evening, Jed found Solomon in the kitchen, wrapping the plates in newspaper and packing them into a cardboard box.

"What are you doing?"

"You no lend me your coffee pot, I no lend you my plates. *Where* you get iron? *Where* you get frying pan?"

For the moment, the "bwana" language was forgotten.

Jed was embarrassed. He looked into Solomon's face and saw only resentment. "This is a serious matter," he said. "Let us sit down and discuss it."

They sat down across the kitchen table from one another. Then the actor in him took over. I would not have attempted what he did, and risked compounding the injury. Somehow, Jed created a transformation. One minute, the two men, master and servant, offender and the injured party, are sitting across the table from one another, deadly serious. The next minute, the two of them are dancing about the kitchen with knives, a long bread knife and a carving knife, whooping and slashing at the air beside one another's heads.

"You bad man! You bad man! I *kill* you! *Aiee!*"

"Don't take the plates! Kill me if you must, but *don't take the plates!*"

Suddenly there is a face at the window. Jed catches sight of it in the middle of a turn, with his knife arm raised high. A hand cupped over the eyebrow, the face peering in through the glass, and then the tap-tap of a car key. Vice-principal Jamieson.

Jed puts down his knife and straightens his clothing. He walks through the living room and opens the front door. Solomon begins quietly unpacking the plates and putting them back on the shelves.

"Jed, er," says Arthur Jamieson, "the Principal has authorized me to speak to you on a matter of . . . visitors." He coughs loudly. "This school does not encourage unmarried masters entertaining overnight visitors of the opposite sex."

Jed stares in amazement.

"Last night," Jamieson's voice is stern and slow, "you were seen driving a young lady in . . . but not out."

"Last night," Jed shouts, with a stupendous frown, "last night, Arthur, I brought Jane Merivale in for a cup of coffee after going with her to the cinema, and then I walked her home to the Girls' School. If you're going to spy on me, you might as well do the job thoroughly!"

Jamieson retreats, mumbling. Jed returns to the kitchen, half angry, half giggling. "God damn it, Mdogo!" He seizes his knife and lunges. Solomon leaps into the air with a loud scream, and the dance continues. In the driveway, Jamieson shakes his head and mutters, then starts his car.

"You clown!" I said, when I heard this tale. "Perfect hams, both of you. You found the right man there."

23

"Solomon?" Jed says. "He is one smart guy, man. You know what he said to Maurice Bowles?" Jed shrinks down to Bwana Mdogo's size. "He said, 'Meester Bowles, how many sheeldren you got?'

"Bowles says, 'I g- I g- I got two children, Mdogo.'" (Jed imitates Maurice Bowles' Lancashire stutter.) "'W- w- why?'

"'How many bicycles?'

"'Th- th- three, Mdogo, w- why?'

"'I got *four sheeldren*, Meester Bowles! And no bicycles. Not *even one* bicycle!'

"Now Solomon's got a bicycle, man. You've seen him riding around on it? Says he's going to send it to his children. At Christmas." Jed broke into a loud, American belly laugh.

"Oh Jed, you might as well stay to dinner," Julia said. She loved his stories. The later it got, the louder and more exaggerated they became. And then of course, the dog. . . .

Jed's experience in theatre was a problem for me. I had just inherited the school's dramatic society from a teacher who'd gone back to England, and I was damned if I was going to give it up. The school had developed a tradition of putting on a Shakespeare every year, using the entire dramatic society in the cast. It was a public event, and got write-ups in the Nairobi newspapers. The dramatic society consisted of a hundred and twenty or a hundred and fifty boys who had signed up for the short-play readings at the start of each year. Putting on a Shakespeare with a cast that size was a challenge that appealed to me. We had multitudes and battle scenes all right! At one performance of *Henry IV, part 1*, when the armies clashed, a woman in the audience got up and ran out of the theatre, shrieking.

Jed helped me with production, of course, but it wasn't the same thing as running the show. "'And *under him,*'" he bellowed, on our living room carpet, shaking his finger at me, "'and under him / My Genius is rebuk'd, as it is said / Mark Antony's was by Caesar.'"

I recognized the quote: Macbeth rationalizing the need to murder Banquo.

"This terr'tory ain't big enough for the two of us, pardner!" I made to blow off his head with my Smith and Wesson. We all laughed, but as usual, the horseplay expressed a truth. I thought of suggesting he take over the short plays, but that was no good. The readings at the beginning of the year were adjudicated, and three or four winners announced, and the winning plays were then produced. But the whole point was for the students to do these productions on their own, and so develop their initiative. The only help we gave them was with costumes. To have Jed take over the production would defeat that main intent.

The problem was solved unexpectedly by the announcement of a new event, the Kenya Schools Drama Festival. Jed leaped at the opportunity. And the first year they won every award, Best Producer, Best Actor and so on. The second year, I forget what happened. The third year was typical Quimby:

It was 1964, the quatercentenary of Shakespeare's birth. Jed came to me, looking serious. "I want to invite you to participate in a project, man. I'm seeking your collaboration."

He wanted to enter a collage called "Shakespeare 400." There would be three scenes, representing the three types of play. For the Histories, he had chosen *Henry V's* Saint Crispin Day speech, and for the Tragedies, a selection from *Julius Caesar*. For the Comedies, he wanted me to produce Falstaff's narration of the robbery, in the Boar's Head Tavern. And all of this within the strict time limits of the Festival's regulations: one rehearsal and one lighting rehearsal at the National Theatre, an hour each: ten minutes to set the stage, and five to strike it; maximum performance time of forty minutes.

"Christ, Jed, aren't you missing something?" I said. "Why not throw in the Sonnets as well, plus maybe a scene from the Dark Comedies. Forty minutes, fellow!"

"I think it can be done, man." (Long, serious pause.) "I want you on board."

"'On board,' hell! Up all night painting scenery is what you mean!"

Jed laughed at the dig. The first time he entered the Festival, he had chosen to stage a Roman comedy in West African dress, set in a village of square mud houses. I had spent the night painting scenery, and even then I didn't finish, and had to continue after class the next day. The Old Man drove down in his Volkswagen at one minute to four, to bid the cast a ceremonial farewell, and had to wait a few minutes while I finished off a wall, which we then hoisted and tied on the roof of the school lorry. "Best of luck!" the Old Man intoned. "Everyone pull his weight! Never mind if you win or lose! Everything done properly!"

Off went the lorry in a cloud of dust, Jed and cast waving, the Old Man standing with arm upraised, like an old Norse king sending warriors to battle. Then he turned to where I stood, paint-spattered, and with bags under my eyes, and he began doing what the students called "stepping." It was his way of expressing rage, and had something to do with blood pressure. He'd lift one foot, then put it down and lift the other, where he stood, stamping in slow motion, his whole body stiff and quivering.

"When you announce at parade . . ." (step; step) " . . . that the lorry will leave at four o'clock, . . ." (step; step) ". . . then it *leaves* at four o'clock! If you mean five past four . . . SAY SO!" He ended with a shout. I stood there numb, as his Volkswagen whined angrily back up the hill.

"JEDEDIAH QUIMBY!" I shouted into the thinning dust, "NEXT TIME MAKE YOUR OWN FUCKING SCENERY!"

But then they came back from the Festival with all the trophies, so what could I say?

Everybody thought "Shakespeare 400" was a wonderful idea. Julia and Mary Greene immediately offered to do the costumes, and my actors were delighted at the chance to revive the Boar's Head scene from last year's production.

Four or five nights in a row, Jed had his casts for *Julius Caesar* and *Henry V* rehearsing past midnight, and not a peep out of Jamieson. When I mentioned scenery, Jed said all I'd need for my scenes was the huge "Boar's Head" sign, and it was true. With a couple of chairs and a table, it created the tavern, and was easily portable.

"What about your two scenes?" I asked.

"I don't know. I need to envisage it."

Our combined casts for the three segments totalled forty boys, plus stage hands, and we knew we could only ask for one trip in the lorry. And of course you couldn't leave the scenery at the National Theatre, so we'd have to bring it with us. It was going to be some trip! I wished Jed would hurry up with envisaging, so that I could plan how to pack it all into the lorry.

At the lighting rehearsal we still had no scenery, so that trip was easy. We were last to rehearse, and the technician asked me to throw the main switch and make sure the doors were locked when we left. It was against the rules to take extra time in the theatre, but I didn't care. Jed was not going to stall any longer, I'd damn well see to that. I went looking for him. I was striding across the lit stage, when suddenly his voice boomed from the dark auditorium, telling me to stand where I was.

"Now move to your left, to your left, TO YOUR LEFT, MAN! Right there! Mark it. How high's the fly there?"

I looked up. "Oh, fourteen feet."

"Write it down, now come forward, FORWARD, TO YOUR RIGHT, there! Mark it. How high?"

Three times this happened, and finally I said, "What the hell are you doing, Jed?"

"For *Henry V* all we need is a big rock, man, there's one out in the parking lot. It's bleak, it's bare, it's like the battle. He puts his foot up on it."

"And what am I marking here?"

"PILLARS, MAN! For *Julius Caesar*. A Roman temple, huh? Great, big, white, marble, *pillars*, man! Fourteen, eighteen, and what did you say, twenty-three feet? It's perfect, it's *strong!* Fluted white marble. Add a couple of feet to those dimensions, because we mustn't be short of the fly. Three tremendous *pillars*, man, rising out of sight!"

I shielded my eyes against the blinding lights and tried to see his face. "Envisaging" was one thing; this was madness. I called out strongly towards his dark outline at the back of the auditorium: "Jed, this is Friday night. We go *on* Monday afternoon. And you're talking about fluted marble pillars that are longer than the school lorry. You're off your cotton-picking rocker, you crazy Yank! You've got to *make* them. And you've got to *carry* them. How are you going to do it?

"Come down here and look, man. It's *strong!* I think it can be done."

I decided to steer clear of the whole project. I was not about to waste a frantic weekend manipulating lengths of bamboo and chicken wire, and *papier mache*, only to have Jed arrive and guffaw. ("That's not *marble*, man, that is *macaroni!*") Perhaps I was in a huff—I don't know. I just rehearsed my actors and kept out of Jed's way, and he didn't come looking for me.

Monday morning, there they were: leaning against the front of the school theatre building, as I crossed the playing field to morning parade. Three gigantic pillars, straight and strong, and gleaming white in the morning sun.

"Who made the pillars for you, Jed?"

"Peter Jones."

"*Peter Jones!* He's the guy that gets me to come over and show him how to jack up his car!"

He builds model airplanes, man. It's the same principle as an airplane fuselage, struts and skin."

They truly were beautiful pillars. They tapered slightly, to enhance the perspective, and later, when they were in place on the stage of the National Theatre, they created exactly the right atmosphere: a sense of public spectacle, of noble men, and traitors. I was impressed—and all the more because the construction was so simple and light. A single stage hand could lift one and put it in place. Peter had used segments of corrugated cardboard, evenly curved, and jointed to look like segments of marble, along frameworks of plywood and lath. He had got them perfectly straight, so they looked heavy and solid. Standing ten feet from one, you'd swear it would stop an ox. In fact, they were so light, there was a danger that an actor might nudge one accidentally and knock it over. We couldn't lash the tops to lighting rails, because of our quick scene changes, so the actors were warned to be extra careful. This slowed the pace of their movements, and in their sweeping togas they aged and became most graceful, which suited the play.

I got the lorry loaded without any problem. The longest pillar overhung the roof, front and back, by several feet, but it was firm. Jed and I packed students into our Morris Minors, and followed the lorry. I had talked to Mwangi, the lorry driver, and said we had lots of time, and he should go slowly and carefully.

It was as though I had not spoken—or had irritated Mwangi and provoked rebellion. He drove the lorry out of the school entrance, but instead of turning left, for the smoother, longer road to town, he swung right, down the short-cut route. He went bucking through switchbacks, and slid into winding, corrugated corners, over potholes and ruts. As I followed, smothered in dust, half-thinking I might overtake him and slow him down, Mwangi stepped on it. We hurtled round a corner into Dagoretti village, and the next thing I knew bodies were flying in the air. One landed with a sickening thud, on the hood of my car.

They were sheep. Mwangi had driven into a herd spread across the road, and had been unable to brake in time. It's a detail that has no apparent connection with Jed Quimby, but whenever I recall the sight of that clotted grey corpse, spinning up in the dust from the two left rear wheels of the overloaded lorry, and landing *thud!* on my car, I think of Jed. It wasn't so much that he was comic himself, but genuinely ludicrous and exaggerated events always seemed to happen around him.

We didn't win everything at the Festival, but we won some. Best Actor, Best Producer, Best Set Design.

I didn't learn from Jed immediately. Perhaps I'm a slow learner, or perhaps my British colonial upbringing had drilled too much moderation into me, and I stood in awe of this American who frowned up projects and then set about accomplishing them. My father taught me how to be polite, and to know my place. From Jed, I learned another kind of life entirely: "envisage" things, and do them; but recognize that always there will be "these grey and unimaginative presences, telling me that I cannot do the things I want to do." In that war of repression which the grey presences wage unceasingly on the creative, a camaraderie grows. So Jed Quimby became a reference point, a major figure in my imagination from my mid-twenties on. He taught me that you have to occupy your own life, stake it out, damn it, and tell the nay-sayers and the trespassers and the parasites to go to hell.

I began to realize what I was learning when I saw Jed deal with his problem of unwanted visitors. Because he had been posted to our school, just outside Nairobi, other Americans from the Teachers for East Africa programme would write and claim friendship. Their postings were out in the boondocks, and they needed to get to town once in a while. Why not pay a visit to Jed Quimby in his three-bedroom house, tootle around Nairobi all day, and come back in time for dinner courtesy of Bwana Mdogo? One of these freeloaders wrote from Uganda announcing his arrival with girlfriend for a three-week stay commencing two days after the letter arrived. "Dear Jed," he wrote, "You may not remember me, but we spoke once in the rain, outside the library, at Makerere. . . ." Jed was enraged.

"What am I going to do, man? Even if I hid out at your place and pretended to be away, they'd simply occupy my house for three weeks. *Listen* to it: "My girlfriend and I will be arriving some time on Friday 22nd to visit with you for three weeks. . . .'"

"What nerve!" I said. "Send the bugger a telegram."

Jed drove to the Post Office and sent it: "NO ROOM IN THE INN STOP QUIMBY."

It worked on that occasion, but he had to find a more permanent solution. "The answer," he said, "is to move. Some place that is literally too small to accommodate people." Fine, but where was there such a house? Jed went looking, and found it. Stuck away behind a hedge was a cottage I had never noticed. A bedroom, a living room, a small dining room, and a bathroom. For years, the place had been lent to the Red Cross, to house a field worker. Right now, it happened to be empty. Best of all, it had a servant's house out back which was larger than the quarters Bwana Mdogo now occupied. They moved in.

"I don't quite see how it's going to work, Jed. Surely your American tourists will insist on sleeping on the dining room floor?"

He looked at me, puzzled, then said, "Oh, you haven't been over since we moved. Come and take a look."

It was marvellous. Jed had been taking piano lessons in Nairobi, and getting quite serious about it, so he had bought a piano. It was a grand. It occupied the little dining room roughly wall to wall. To enter the room, you had to crawl between the piano's legs.

"How the hell did you get it in here?"

"We had to make some adjustments," he said, and did not elaborate.

That was the end of Jed's unwanted visitors. His real friends, when they came, slept anywhere a body could fit. And mice made nests in his underwear and socks, but what can you expect in an old house hidden behind a cypress hedge? Jed was happy there, and might have stayed forever. He was a good American all right, and brought his music, drama, basketball and a dozen other contributions to the school. I notice in the school's official history, Arthur Jamieson has shrunk my own time there in half, and attributed all my main achievements to Jed. Touché. "Under him / My Genius is rebuk'd." To be honest, I don't care. It's quite appropriate that Jed should have my measly honours attached to his own. His was always the larger, more inventive imagination. Even the Old Man knew that. The Old Man might have relied on me to fix a visiting team's lorry, but for Jed he had the respect owed to an artist.

I'll never forget an incident one morning at parade. The Old Man had been to visit Jed's class, to evaluate his teaching, and had had nothing bad to say; but he did point out in a friendly way that Jed had misused a word. He had told the class that the Old Man was their friend, and also his friend, and therefore their "mutual friend." The Old Man said this usage was incorrect: two parties may have a third party as their "common" friend, but "mutual" means reciprocal between the two. Jed argued, and cited the Dickens title. The Old Man slipped Fowler's *Modern English Usage* into Jed's mailbox to settle the point—the page was marked with a slip of paper. Now, at parade, with the Old Man looking formal and donnish, despite his khaki shorts and bush jacket, Jed handed back Fowler with a note. "Sir," it said, "You were right, and I was wrong. You are not our 'mutual friend.' You are 'common.'" The Old Man cracked up and had to hold his forehead to still the laughs, before three hundred serious students and a dozen staff.

After I left Kenya, Jed stayed on for a couple of years. From time to time, we corresponded, ten years of letters, with theatrical gesturing and crude cartoons. Once, when he had moved back to New Hampshire, and I wrote to say I might be passing by, he sent a Xeroxed cartoon entitled "Shower." Underneath, in Jed's unmistakable scrawl: "I think we can offer you superb accommodations here." The picture shows a naked man scrubbing his back with a long-handled brush, and pissing a fat stream down onto an

electric fan which is showering it back on him.
The years passed, and we met. Then came another ten
years of letters, and drawings, and cartoons. Once I sent
him a story I had written, and he wrote back dismissing my
"literary posturings." Once he wrote a poem, and sent it in
to *Atlantic* magazine, and when he didn't hear from them
in a few days, he took the bus to Boston, and knocked on
the door at 8 Arlington Street, to find out what the editors
had decided. I wrote telling him he was extremely naïve.
We both went through divorces and marriages and other
relationships, problems over children, and contemplations
over the state of civilization. Our letters reflect it all. We
met again, then once again, and sat around the fire telling
stories to one another's latest companions. "Shakespeare
400" and the pillars, how Bwana Mdogo got his bicycle. . . .
The laughter hasn't changed, and after the first few hours
of meeting again, it's all talked out. The relationship will go
on like this forever, I suppose.

Our women friends are puzzled, a bit jealous, perhaps.
"Why don't you and Jed just get it on together?" one said to
me. And, another: "You won't do things for *me* when I ask,
but you'd bend over backwards for Jed. What *is* it about
you two?"

This riled me, and I went to the file of his letters, which I
have never thrown away. I found one letter in which he
refers to me marking student essays in the staff room in
Kenya. "You were able to sit there and get the goddamned
papers marked, while the rest of the faculty was exchang-
ing ridiculous gossip. I envied you your concentration, that
you could isolate yourself in a public space and achieve
your objectives." It's himself he's talking about, not me. I've
always been distracted by any fly on the window.

In another letter he writes this: "The happiest and best
relationships, am I wrong?, seem to be those in which the
roles are not constantly being renegotiated but which have
been defined, not perhaps fairly, but defined, and the thing
works, like a hinge on a gate, it functions."

I picked up the phone and called Jed. I hadn't seen him in two years, and because he never bothers to relate the details that are mundane to him, but necessary information to others (like job, or companion, or birth, or death) I couldn't picture his life. And I wanted to know, right away. It was midnight, and I was drinking wine. I dialled, thinking "Three a.m. in New Hampshire—so what," and got the "number-not-in-service" tape.

"Oh shit, he's not dead is he?" The last I knew he was happily in love, and was working his butt off for an environmental agency that even paid him a little.

Information had another number, so I called it, and he answered on the third ring. He sounded muffled, drugged.

"Are you all right?" I said.

"No man, I'm not all right."

"What's the matter?"

"Anh," he said. "Anh, man, why don't you put your phone down and let me call you back. I'd like to talk to you."

"Go ahead and talk," I said.

"I mean a long time. Maybe an hour."

I said, "Talk."

He said he was exhausted, terribly tired. That's why he had sounded drugged. Everything had gone wrong, and he was losing the war on every front. The grey presences were winning.

"I'm forty-two years old, man! I don't have a relationship, I don't have a house, I don't have a job, and I don't have any money."

"Where are you now?"

"You know where I am. I'm in New Hampshire. *You* phoned *me*, man."

"Jed, where are you *living?*"

He brushed the question off and started telling me again about his father's death. I asked again, and he brushed me off and told me all his friends had "crapped out" on him. He said I was the only person in the world with whom he could claim friendship.

"That's only because I'm four thousand miles away," I said. If I was there, you'd probably say I'd crapped out too."

Jed laughed, for the first time.

"Where are you *living?*"

"Man, anh, I'm living . . . in a room. A decent couple. They paint their fence. I rent a room in their house, and they're sleeping in their bedroom down the hallway. They have a garden. With rose bushes. You get the picture?"

"Hmm. Listen, Jed, think hard and try to tell me one thing in your life you'd like to change right now."

First he said he'd like a job. Then he said that wasn't the problem; he'd like to have a sense of direction, for the future.

"Well, Jed, you quit teaching because the Vice-principal took the doors off the girls' can so he could look under and see they weren't spending too long standing in the cubicles."

"Do you *believe* that, man! I am *not* going back into teaching. It's all about repression, and they're probably still doing it—goddamn flag in every classroom."

I felt I had him on the assertive.

"All right, Jed, so where is your project? Theatre? Environment? Politics? What's it to be?"

"Listen, man, I'll tell you something. I always find a project, that's not a problem." He spoke rapidly, and his voice rose. "It's not my father's death, or a job, *you know what it is?*" It was as though we were back years ago in Africa, Jed pacing back and forth on the living room carpet, and the dog going at his ankles.

"The problem is, I like to FUCK!"

"Well of course, Jed, but—"

"I mean, I LIKE TO FUCK SOMEONE WHO LIKES TO FUCK!"

"Sure, but—"

"SOMEONE WHO LIKES TO FUCK *ME!*"

I imagined the decent couple's eyes, bulging wide as

soupspoons into the darkness of their bedroom.

"Jed," I said. "Listen, is there a dog there?"

"What do you mean?"

"Is it barking?"

He laughed his big American belly laugh.

"Listen," he said. "I've got a story to tell you. . . ."

The hinge was on the gate, and working fine.

NORTH BURNABY,
THE HERDSMAN, AND FREUD

It's imperative that I talk to Freud. You may think this unnecessarily picky of me, given the range and sophistication of modern help available, but I have my very good reasons. I lift up the phone and call his office in the Fairmont Medical Building. His receptionist has an accent that I can't quite identify on the phone. Swiss? Belgian? We set a date for the appointment.

As I walk into the office, she is preoccupied with her word-processor, and does not look up. She is singing along quietly to the Country & Western lyric emerging from a small plastic transistor radio on her desk:

Quand le soleil dit bonjour aux montagnes
Je suis seul
Je ne veux penser q'a toi.

I hear it now: she's French, from France.

"Nashville," I say, *"mais Nashville-sur-Dordogne?"*

She flashes me a weak smile, and buzzes on the intercom. After a minute or two, the inner door opens, and there stands Freud, just as in the photographs, his granny glasses reflecting like tiny round mirrors. He looks down at the small card his secretary hands him. "'Alis-tair' he says frowning. "'-air'? Auf '-er'?"

"It's the Scottish spelling," I say.

"So! Schottisch!" he says brightly.

"But that was a long time ago," I say. "We've been several generations in Africa."

"Africa! Ouf." Freud sighs, and rolls his eyes, as from a low blow. "Perhaps you should be consulting my colleague Doktor Jung."

"No, no!" I say. "You are the one who broke the unconscious to us. Since then, the rest of it all seems déjà vu."

Freud lifts his eyebrows, and carefully repositions a green china rabbit on his desk. My compliment has pleased him. I sense we are off to a good start. And he confirms this by making his idea of a joke: he leans toward me confidentially, and in a thick German caricature, he says, "Komm sie in! Vee in Englisch zen vill schpeak." And he laughs aloud. He sits me down and makes me comfortable. "So begin," he says.

*

"Should I tell you about Gladys Brown and her mother? No, later."

First I tell him about Mbarara, Uganda. How Julia and I drove there in 1962 to visit another couple. He was a teacher in the high school, newly out from Scotland. They had visited us in Nairobi, and stayed a few days, and this was a reciprocal visit. The four of us did little else but play bridge, and drink beer, and eat, or sometimes Steve and I would go off and play golf. Every day the same empty routine. One day I drove down to the Post Office for stamps, and stood nervously in line. Uganda had just become independent, and you never knew when somebody might take vicious exception to you as a white: people had been deported from the country on twenty-four hours' notice for some real or imagined insult. Twenty-four hours to dispose of your house and car, pack up, and be on a plane. The black clerk looked down the lineup to me, the solitary white, standing ten or twelve places back.

"Yes, can I help you?" he called over the top of the wicket.

I smiled sheepishly, and tried to indicate with a quieting hand motion that I was happy to wait my turn.

"YES SUH! CAN I HELP YOU?"

I put on an affable grin, and waited in line. ("God!" I thought, "What if they find out I'm from Kenya?"—which was then still a British colony, and my car parked alone, slap outside the Post Office, with its giveaway EA(K) international plate.)

"Akili nusu huyu, labda," said one clerk to the other, and I grinned on, pretending not to understand the Swahili ("Maybe he's not all there.")

"The town seems very tranquil," I said, when I made it back, relieved, to Steve and Morag's house.

"Aye, it's actually been calmer since Independence than it was before. Everyone's perfectly friendly."

Although it sits some distance back from the national boundaries, Mbarara is really a border town. You go south to Tanzania, Ruanda, and Burundi, or west to the Congo. In '62, there were still quite a few bullet-ridden American cars with Congo plates, abandoned at the roadside and stripped, their Belgian owners . . . who knows where? And later, in the seventies: put yourself there, seeing through the wide-open eyes of a small child hiding in the bush, watching, as the camouflaged Tanzanian troop carriers come rolling through, load after load of the big, smiling soldiers who've crossed the border, with the secret complicity of the big powers, to put an end to Idi Amin's barbarian dictatorship. Listen to the doof-doof-doof of their guns as, lacking provisions of their own, they shoot anything on four legs that looks edible—later grinding their half-track armoured cars up into the national parks, against peppery resistance from the remaining game wardens, and exterminating elephant, hippopotamus, rhino . . . . As the small child, of course, you do not see all this happening in front of your eyes. But the hopeless feeling in your belly is the same as if you had. Oh yes, to tell the history of a place like Mbarara you resort to cliche: it's a landscape soaked in blood.

Yet the four young foreigners sit playing bridge, while the servant sings quietly to himself at the ironing table.

"Gosh, this beer's a bit flat isn't it? Never mind, I'll take it back to Manubhai later this afternoon, and he'll give us a new case—he's very good about that sort of thing. Three no trump!"

"Really Steve? All right, four spades!"

Just before we left Mbarara on that visit, I read a dramatic story in the paper. A bus, on the Mbarara-Kampala road, ran into a herd of cows, and killed one. The herdsman opened the door of the bus, stepped in, and "speared the driver to death." In many parts of Africa there are prices for accidents like that. There's a set range of compensation, and usually after an hour or so of haggling, the money is paid, and everybody goes on their way. I've heard a certain African country described as "one main road with houses down the length of each side," and the "joke" about the poor family whose children are sent to push chickens and goats into the path of oncoming vehicles. No such "joke" in this case.

Imagine that herdsman. His cows are his life. Fifteen kilometres away they've burned off the grass, and the fresh green shoots are springing up nicely. He's moving his herd there slowly, taking a couple of days at it. There are drawn-out conversations with villagers on the way. A woman offers him an aluminum beaker of milk, steeped with charcoal. He enters her hut briefly for a little "road fun," then moves on to catch up with his animals. The sun is hot, but there are good, solid clouds in the sky, and life's not bad at all. The rich, familiar stench of cowdung in the dust. The herder puts his fingers in his mouth and gives off several high, alarming whistles to head in a straggler, and the cow responds with a moan and a slow turn. White tick birds move off one animal's hump to graze on another's.

Suddenly the blare of the horn, squealing rubber, the slamming sound, the cow stretched out obscenely in the roadway. The great wide Mercedes Diesel bus, throbbing and stinking, its radiator grille smashed in. The herdsman moves into action. Imagine that spear! One of those two-and-a-half metre Maasai things, all metal blade and counter-weight, with a few centimetres of wooden shaft in the mid-dle to hold it by. Up the steps he goes, and "spears the dri-ver to death" without a word, retrieving directly, his hand never letting go of his weapon. Already, villagers have con-gregated, and begin dragging the dead cow to the grass. Women have gone to their huts to fetch pangas and karais, and are making their way back to the cow, to cut it up once the dickering is all over. The herdsman's face is a wretched scowl. He lifts his spear aloft and whistles, to sig-nal his remaining cattle over the road to safety. *"Killed my cow! You dead man!"*

Now the passengers are stirring. Men stand urinating at the roadside, and conversing loudly. Others wander over to survey the preparations for butchering. The herdsman keeps apart with his herd, scowling and thinking of the happier time before the accident, but local men pursue him, speaking loudly, and thrusting their hands as they insistently try to negotiate the price of the meat. This nickle-and-dimeing will take a long time to settle to every-one's satisfaction—headmen and elders may still be presid-ing over arguments a year or more from now. But the main retribution is over and done with, at least in the herdsman's mind. *Umeuwa 'ngombe yangu—utakufa!* Killed my cow, you're dead! If there's more "justice" to come, he isn't thinking about that. Meanwhile, the victim of the herds-man's rage lies open-eyed, back where he fell in the dri-ver's seat. A couple of passengers have taken a look, to check that there's no sign of life. Now the corpse is avoid-ed. Two kilometres away at an Indian *duka* a small boy has arrived breathless with the news, and the *duka* owner is cranking his telephone handle, long-short-short-short-long, the party line call of the police post. The bus, empty now except for the baggage on the roof and the corpse in the driver's seat, blocks the road, and traffic negotiates slowly around it. Someone has switched off the idling motor.

*

Silence. Freud shows no reaction to my story, except to write.

"And when did you first become aware of the unconscious?" he asks me without looking up. He is writing, writing, writing, on a buff-coloured pad. His pencil keeps making little tears in the cheap paper.

It was in Cape Town that I first read Freud, years and years ago. I was seventeen, and two years before that I had had a very disturbing experience with Aldous Huxley in northern Kenya: I had been reading *Brave New World* and there were these allusions to free sex—people just meeting in elevators and agreeing to go and do it with the casual air of racquetball players today, who pick names and phone numbers off a "ladder" in the Community centre. People carried contraceptives and admired the styles of one another's pouches. Men discussed whether a certain woman was "pneumatic" to ride on, or not. I was so disgusted by all this, that I took the book, walked into the kitchen with it, and before the astonished gazes of three or four servants, I inserted the handle into the hotplate, and lifted it out, and dropped *Brave New World* into the coals of the woodstove, and turned without a word, and marched back to my bedroom.

"*Ala! Kumbe mtoto ya wazungu anachoma kitabu!*" said the cook in amazement, behind my back, "What the hell would the white kid want to burn a book for?"

But now, in the cold winter of Cape Town, during the July university holiday, I was all alone, in a rented house

42

on Dean Street. No servants, and my house-mates had all gone home for the holiday, one to Southern Rhodesia, one to East London, one just locally to Paarl. And I was reading Freud's *Interpretation of Dreams*. On the bedroom wall was a calendar, with a curvaceous pinup. Liz Taylor, nineteen years old, with breasts to die for, and a smile that turned my brains to mush. At night, I dreamed incredible dreams, and then, in my dreams, I started interpreting the meanings even before I woke up. My house-mate from Paarl had brought in some farmer sausage, *boerewors,* and it hung drying on a string in the kitchen. I dreamed of my penis hanging down out the bottom of my shorts, and meeting a beautiful woman on the street, and being dreadfully embarrassed. And then it started getting an erection, and I tried to hide it behind a lamp-post. But she took me by the hand, and led me into a room with a sloping floor.

In the morning, I walked up to the University library, and found a copy of *Scouting for Boys*. I sat guiltily at the huge green-surfaced reading table, with a serious, scholarly frown on my face, and looked up again Baden Powell's advice about sex: "Don't make love to a woman unless you mean to marry her. Don't marry a woman unless you have a sufficient income to support her and two or three children." I wanted to take the book home with me, for security, but I was too embarrassed to go through the check-out procedure. Scouting was always a foreign thing to us, a kind of sissy game for English wets.

I went home, and wrote a long letter to my father, explaining that my life up to now had all been fake, but that from now on I was going to be real. My life was going to be the roots and branches of the tree, not just the leaves. I mailed the letter, and then went through a couple of weeks of agony, wishing I had not done so. When his answer came back, the only thing he picked up on was my mention that I had started smoking a pipe.

"I have no objection to your smoking a pipe in moderation," he wrote, "if it helps you study, and provided your hockey captain agrees."

When my house-mates came back, I showed one of them the letter, and he smiled.

"Imagine going up to du Toit and saying, 'Excuse me, Piet, but do you mind if I smoke a pipe, in moderation?' The look he would give you!"

When the Michaelmas term started, I was too busy preparing for exams to worry any further about Freud. If I dreamed at all, censorship, which had begun when I analyzed the dreams within the dream, exerted itself even more strongly. By morning, I would recall nothing.

*

Freud writes and writes. He has laid his arm across the pad, whether for his own comfort or to exclude my looking, I don't know.

"Shall I go on?"

"A moment please," he says. He writes a couple more sentences, stops, scratches his mustache. "I don't think you've mentioned your mother?"

"No."

"All right, go on. Someone called Gladys Brown?"

She was a beautiful girl. She lived in North Burnaby, and was a member of one of my graduate seminars at UBC. She began flirting with me one day, about six months after my marriage to Julia had broken up. I don't remember the words, but I remember the jolliness of her voice, a kind of high-energy Canadian teasing. My friends in the seminar all mocked her because she was not a graduate like us but an undergrad education student, and the education faculty at UBC was the campus joke, the "mouse house" (after Mickey).

"Do you believe creativity is culturally determined?" Gladys asked us one day, before the prof arrived in the seminar room. "I have to do a paper."

"What *is* creativity, Gladys?" someone asked.

"Oh *don't* be like that! Come on, you guys. Do you think creativity is culturally determined, or not? I've only got a week."

I was living at that time in a basement suite at Wilma Vance's house. I was driving home one day, and offered Gladys a ride, and then she asked to see my place.

"Oh, my! This is nice," she said, casting her bright eyes around my dingy rooms. I made her tea, and showed her pictures of my children. She coo-ed and bubbled, and filled me with a kind of innocent joy that I had not known in a long time. So I started to invite her out—not on dates, but to go fishing. I'd pick her up at her parents' at four or five in the morning, and we'd drive to Weaver Lake, or Birkenhead, or even, once, five hundred kilometres round trip to Alleyne Lake, just for a day's fishing. Out on the lake, her bubbliness would all be gone. She lay tranquil in the boat, enjoying it. Normally she used a lot of make-up and false eyelashes and dazzling earrings, but when we went fishing, there was none of that. She was just a natural, quiet girl, little more than a child, and she kept me company through some talk and some long silences. One night, before I took her home we stopped at my place to eat some of the kokanee we'd caught. After supper, we kissed. And then we lay on my bed, and kissed some more, and undressed one another. She was a virgin, and wanted me to put an end to that, but I just couldn't do it. I came between her thighs, like a young Kikuyu lover, but I just couldn't bring myself to enter her, and she was disappointed.

One night, she came to dinner, together with Wilma Vance and her then husband, and some other friends. We told fishing stories, and I got out a gang-troll and showed it to them, holding it stretched out in front of me, and shaking it to make all the silver willow leaves spin around, the way they do in the water, to attract the fish. Wilma said to me afterwards, "That Gladys is a real gang-troll with all her make-up and her false eyelashes."

"I like her," I said.

"*Well*, she likes you! Watch out, Alistair. That one's trying to swim right into your net!"

"She wants me to go to bed with her," I said.

"No doubt!"

"I can't do it," I said. "Her *first* lover? Surely it should be someone who loves her?"

"I thought you said you liked her."

"Yeah, I *like* her."

So Gladys and I went fishing once in a while. They were little innocent Wordsworthian idylls in the midst of our own personal struggles. Then one day, I went to pick her up to go to a movie, and I had to wait while she finished getting ready. I sat in the living room talking to her mother while Gladys fussed with her makeup.

"Well, I got that neighbour of mine today!" said Mrs Brown, with a smug smile.

"How?"

"They have this dog, you see. They got it fourteen years ago, as a puppy. And it began coming over and doing its business in our yard. Well, I spoke to them about it, but nothing happened. Every other day you'd look out on the lawn and there'd be this dog mess. I'd have to go and hose it away."

"Good for the grass!" I said.

"No, but I mean *fourteen years!* And when it was just a little puppy they were nothing. But now that it's old, they're—oh just disgusting, big, you know, and full of— oogh!"

"So what did you do?"

"I got this apple box from the supermarket. And every day, I went out there, and scooped it up with a garden trowel. Little by little, I filled that box, and kept it in the garage. Two months, it took. And this morning, before it was light, I went over and dumped it on their front step."

"You did! All over their front step? Did you ring the bell?"

"No, no. I mean I just left the box there. They're bound to know who did it. But they can't say a thing."

Suddenly, a wave of resistance comes over me.

"You know," I say, "that's not the way we do things in Africa. You know what happens in Africa? You see a guy's dog come over and shit on your lawn, eh?"

I see Mrs Brown wince at the word "shit." I get to my feet, and begin acting out the story compulsively. I can't even hear her reaction now. There's no stopping me.

"You see his dog come and take a crap, and you go out there and start shouting. 'Eh! EH!!' And when the neighbour comes out of his house, you shout, 'EH! YOU!! Come and look here, your dog's shitting all over my lawn!' Vaguely I am aware that the accent I have adopted doesn't sound African at all. It sounds more Italian than anything, but I can't help it, I have to go on with the story.

"Pretty soon there's an argument, huh? A crowd gathers. They block the road. The school bus can't get through. A national holiday is declared: the day of the dogshit! Everybody goes down to the pub. That's the way we deal with things like that in Africa, Mrs Brown."

Gladys has emerged from the bathroom, and is standing watching my performance with a surprised look. Her contact lenses shine brightly, and her long dark lashes blink and flutter.

"Let's get going, Monsieur!" she says with a nervous laugh. "You'll give my mother a heart attack, with all that yelling."

After that night, I didn't see any more of Gladys Brown— or her mother.

*

Watching Freud's pencil violating the paper, I wonder what the hell happens to all these notes. Am I dictating his next book for him? Is that what that woman is doing out front with the word-processor, taking all Freud's patient-notes and marketing them? Freud's face is impassive, his hand firm, just the distant wave-like sound of the graphite moving on the paper, and the occasional *skrik, skrik* when he tears it. I feel so helpless before him. What order or meaning is he perceiving? I'm frustrated to the point of rage. I want to pick up his stupid china rabbit and shatter it on his desk in a million pieces.

Freud smiles, as though reading my mind. He puts down his pencil and breathes out deeply.

"So?" I say.

"So," he replies, and looks down at his joined fingers. I wait. He's not going to say any more?

Just as my patience is running out, he opens his mouth again:

"Drive carefully," he advises. "And practise safe sex."

SPEARS

"*Avete viatores!* Permit me to enquire: *de qua provincia aestuosa rei publicae* might you hail?"

The voice was southern English. We were in the Roman baths at Pompeii, and the young English tourist was hamming it up for his three companions. He was lying spread-eagled in the restored tiled bath, in khaki shorts and bush jacket, his head up like a three-month baby's. He was high on travel, playing into the history of the site, asking where in the far-flung empire we came from.

"*De qua provincia?*" I said. "*De provincia aestuosa Keniae.* Though I wouldn't say *aestuosa*'s the word. 'Sultry'? No. The Coast maybe, but upcountry it's quite temperate."

"Good grief you speak English. I took you for Italians!"

"Italians don't have turnup cuffs on the bottom of their pants," I said. "And many of them speak English too."

He scrambled out at once and began pumping my hand. "Nigel Rawsthorne, old boy. I say, what a bloody miracle, you're not really from Kenya are you. Chaps, chaps, our friends here are from *Kenya!* Of *all* the coincidences!"

His manner was so excessive that I regretted having

answered him in the first place.

"But we're *go*-ing there, old boy! It's our final destin-*ation!* What luck! Do let's find a bar."

I won't say we were dragged against our will. We had not spoken English for weeks, except to one another, and even the most obnoxious people can become interesting when you know you're never going to see them again. After the introductions, we agreed to go and eat with them in a trattoria in Naples, and answer their questions about Kenya, and hear their story. They were funded by a British beer maker to travel through southern Europe, certain parts of the Middle East, and down the Nile to East Africa on an advertising junket. They had thousands of miniature bottles of beer to distribute from the back of a long-wheelbase Land Rover provided for them by the company, and plastered with its logo.

"That's all we have to do, you see, and for that we get our trip more or less paid for."

"But I'm curious how the opportunity arose. Why would the company give you the money—is it a family connection?"

"Nothing of the sort. We had to sell ourselves to them. Standard business procedure: attract attention, inspire belief, intensify desire, then motivate the buying action. It's called the Sanford Advertising Technique old boy. Sanford's an American, they're rather clever at these things."

"But how did you go about it," I asked, "attracting attention and so forth?"

Nigel Rawsthorne closed one eye. His other pierced mine across the table. "We have a special feature which ensures that we get our pictures in the newspapers."

"And what's that?"

"We're the tiddlywinks champions of the world," he said.

Someone laughed.

Later, in our tent at the Solfatara campsite, Julia said, "Those people are an absolute write-off."

But I was struck with them. Young, hearty, filled with

mindless aristocratic laughter, they were exactly the sort of Englishmen and women my father despised with a bitter scorn: despised, and bitched about them constantly at the dinner table—and hired them. From Oxford and Cambridge and the London Inns of Court, he hired them into his law firm in Nairobi, complaining all the while about "the bond": the Immigration Department had a regulation forcing employers of expatriates to deposit a bond equivalent to first class airfare back to the country of origin, in case they didn't work out.

"That's what gets me, Father growled. "First class! I have never travelled first class in my life and I don't expect to. But we bring one of these young toffs out here, and discover after a month that the only thing he knows how to do is put his feet up on the desk and read the newspaper. So we sack him. And lo and behold, he flies home first class at our expense. This last one had the cheek to send us a bill for extra baggage!"

"Did you pay it?" my brother asked.

"No darned fear, I wrote him a stinker!"

In retrospect, I doubt it. My father often promised tough action, but seldom followed through. I heard my grandmother once accuse him: "You! Just like your father. Big talk at home in front of the women, but when you go back to the office it's all peace and politeness."

So, that night in the little tent at Solfatara, after Julia had written off our new acquaintances, I lay thinking about them, and about my father's ambiguous attitude toward the English toffs: hired them for their class and polish, but personally despised them. Even the ones who didn't get fired for laziness and incompetence and sent home first class, even the ones that "took" with the firm, and made it in Nairobi's post-war economic boom, and bought houses in Spring Valley and Lower Kabete, and imported huge, shiny Daimlers and Rolls Royces, even with them, my father's irrepressible good humour and chitchat didn't fool me. Deep in the heart of him, he hated their guts. He would sit in his chair in our living room, with a bunched up mouth, listening to me blab on about becoming a professional actor, his thumbs automatically rubbing at the fabric, and the distant regard on his face as plain as a book: *You must go for Law, boy, and that'll be one fewer of these damned Limeys we need to import.*

I imagined trying to tell him the story of this encounter: a young Limey toff spread-eagled in the bath in Pompeii, mistaking Julia and me for Italians. "The tiddlywinks champions of the world." Forget it! I couldn't even make a funny story out of it. Better not try.

What was it, then, that I found so attractive about Nigel Rawsthorne and his girlfriend Mandy, and the two other couples travelling halfway round the world in a Land Rover, distributing miniature bottles of beer?

"Who's the most successful man you know in Nairobi?" Nigel had asked me across the table in the *trattoria*.

I was twenty-one. I had never thought of things like that. "Successful?"

Nigel, also about twenty one, swirled a quarter-filled glass of red wine, and rocked in his chair. "Successful at making money," he said.

Names came to mind: Jack Block, Dalgety, Suleiman Virjee, whoever owned the Motor Mart? John Grant? The Hughes of Hughes and Company?

"Honestly, Nigel, I haven't a clue.

"We were *ho*-ping," said Mandy, in a voice that made me think of apples and private school, "it might be *poss*-ible to make an ascent of Kilimanjaro."

"That's certainly possible," I said. "I've done it myself."

She was wearing thin khaki safari pants like you see nowadays on mannequins displaying Italian designs, but which in those days, the early sixties, you'd have had to buy from a safari outfitter. She was blonde, and had a scent of jasmine about her, and she didn't talk much; but she had intelligent eyes, and I felt there was something being held in reserve. When Nigel shrugged off my refusal to name the very wealthy of Nairobi, I began to dismiss him. But Mandy's blue eyes and khaki-clad body lived on for a while in my memory. I never expected to see them again.

But they really were the tiddlywinks champions of the world! I'd thought he was joking, and everyone just laughed when he said it. Six months later, back in Kenya, there they were on the front page of the *East African Standard*, posed beside the back of the Land Rover, holding beer miniatures, grinning. Underneath, the caption read: "Mr. Nigel Rawsthorne and Miss Amanda Woods, Tiddlywinks Champions of the World, issue a challenge to all comers from Kenya, Uganda and Tanganyika, for a three-game match, to be played by International Rules, at a cold and most unlikely venue!"

In the story, the reporter said surely the tiddlywinks was a gimmick! Did they really expect to get any takers?

No gimmick at all, Nigel explained. Originally they had made the title up, but when they had their publicity pictures taken in London and distributed to the press, they received a stern letter from the Bedfordshire Tiddlywinks Club, asking if they were aware of the existence of the International Tiddlywinks League, and threatening to sue.

"We had no alternative but to challenge the top three teams according to League rules, and win the title formally. In the end, we managed to squidge our way to victory!" said Nigel.

And now, as the new champions, they had the right to refuse any challenge, until the challenger had beaten numbers two and three. But they also had the option to issue an open challenge under conditions of their own choice. "We're inviting anyone who thinks they can beat us to take us on—on the top of Mount Kilimanjaro."

I showed Julia the paper, and she read it with a face pulled between disdain and amusement. She handed the paper back to me without saying a word.

A few days later, I walked into the Staff Room at break,

and there sat Nigel Rawsthorne. He jumped to his feet, and shook my hand vigorously.

"Alistair! I need your help, old boy. It's critical."

"Oh, what's the matter?" I asked, with a sinking heart.

"I barely know you, and yet I feel you're the only fellow in the country I can ask to be my best man."

"You and Mandy are getting married?"

"Mandy? No, old boy, I'm marrying someone you know—someone whose family knows yours." He named a prominent Nairobi lawyer, from a rival firm to my father's. The man had two or three farms, a big practice, and connections to the English peerage.

"Which daughter?" I asked.

"Nicola."

"You lucky devil!" She was a brilliant, outgoing girl with a beautiful face, and a figure that made men look away sheepishly.

During the wedding rehearsal, while Nicola's mother walked around estimating how many arum lilies it would take to fill All Saints' Cathedral, Nigel got into an argument with the minister. Canon Lesser said that the bride and groom should bow their heads during the solemn blessing of the marriage; instead, Nigel proposed that they hold hands and look into one another's eyes. I saw Nicola's mother, returning to the group, smile with admiration at his assertiveness.

"It is *customary* to bow the *heads,*" Canon Lesser insisted. You may see it done otherwise in American pictures, but that is the rite of the Church of England."

"Ah, but does it actually specify as much in the *Book of Common Prayer?*" asked Nigel.

The clergyman sighed. "Oh if you wish it very much," he snapped quickly.

"I happen to think it's most important, sir," Said Nigel. "Symbolic, as it were."

The wedding was one of the social events of the year,

and was extensively covered by the press. Both the *Kenya Weekly News* and the *East African Standard* even mentioned the joke I told before my toast to the bridesmaids. The *Illustrated London News* ran a group picture. I felt elated by my contact with the world of the rich.

We thought we had managed the going-away well. It was the custom to booby-trap the car, so we had parked a decoy Ford Zephyr in an easy place to find, behind a bougainvillaea. Nigel's Austin we had hidden in a stable. To make doubly sure, we had left the new Rover, their wedding present from Nicola's parents, which was the car they were actually taking on honeymoon, parked at my house twenty-five kilometres away. But nobody fell for the decoy. They found Nigel's Austin and filled the trunk with water, and sprayed the insides of the windows with Blanco, and wrote "Just Married" with toothpaste; they tied all kinds of junk underneath, put stones in the hubcaps, rolled small potatoes down the exhaust pipe and rammed a big one on the end.

Nigel and Nicola rumbled down the tarmac driveway with the Austin sounding like a WWII tank, spilling a steady sheet of water, and firing on two cylinders. The big potato shot off the tailpipe at the perfect moment, just as they rounded the hedge and disappeared from the waving, cheering crowd. It was as though Nigel had fired a parting shot at his disappointed rivals. The next day, returning the Austin, I stopped and opened the hood to see why the engine was misfiring so very badly, and found that someone had laid an arum along the tops of the plugs, and an electrical storm of crackling blue sparks was shorting out through the lily's stem.

The weekend after the wedding, Julia had a cold, so I went alone to a party in Kileleshwa, and there I bumped into Mandy. She was wearing the same khaki outfit she had had on in Pompeii.

"You really are a knockout!" I said.

"I hear you were splendid at Nigel's wedding," she said.

"I would have come, but I was too busy trying to make arrangements to get down to Loitokitok."

"Why are you going *there?*"

"To climb Kilimanjaro. We were going to play tiddly-winks, you remember, but nobody took us on. It's something I'd like to do before I go home, only we no longer have the Land Rover."

"You're going with the Outward Bound? They have transportation."

"No, no."

"Alone?"

"Yes."

"How are you proposing to get down there?"

"Well, I was hoping to arrange for a lift with a District Officer, but now that's fallen through I'll just have to hike in and hope for a ride."

I laughed.

"Mandy," I said. "You don't know what you're talking about. Even by car it's two or three hours, and the road's appalling. You could stand there all day with your thumb out, but nobody'd come. No one drives down there. And you can't possibly walk it. The area is full of lions and leopards."

"Oh, I'll be all right," she said, with a lovely smile.

All my Galahad instincts surfaced at the thought of this soft and innocent English girl, alone and bewildered on the thorny, dry Kajiado plains, watched by patient carnivores.

"Please don't do it," I said in a quiet voice. "Take the bus down to Moshi, and climb it from the Tanganyika side at Marangu. There's a hotel there, and guides, and huts to sleep in on the mountain. It takes three days up. That's the way I did it. Believe me, Loitokitok's impossible—and really dangerous to try."

She smiled. She put her finger on my nose and said in rabbit talk: "Big bwuvver not wowwy so much," and walked away to another group at the party, leaving the scent of jasmine on my face.

Twenty-five years later, I am taking the ferry to the Gulf Islands from Vancouver to go and house-sit for Wilma Vance, and feed her chickens. I am walking up the ramp at Sturdies Bay, when I hear a voice behind me declaiming: *"Nemo insula est, sibi sat."*
I glance around. "No man is an island entire of itself." Nigel Rawsthorne. Forty-six years old and paunchy. I look at the woman beside him. Her youthful beauty has only slightly decayed. The skin around her mouth has creases. Mandy.
It takes me a full minute, walking along the ramp, to remember even roughly the next line of the Donne, and force it into shaky Latin. I turn and say:
"Sumus quisque eius continentis frustum, illae terrae pars. Every man is a piece of the continent, a part of the main."
"Christ!" says Nigel. "And . . . if ever I go to Australia and say something in fifth form Latin, will I find you there *too?* I have no doubt!"
I wanted to hear their news, so I invited them to come up and have dinner with me, and they arrived the next day just as I was giving the chickens their afternoon feed.
"What fat hens!" cried Mandy. "Do they lay well?"
"I'll give you some eggs," I said. "Real eggs again. They'll remind you of Africa."
We drank wine while I barbecued a salmon, and we ate and then sat and talked.
Nigel's marriage to Nicola had lasted three years, ending in an amicable divorce. "I found I never really wanted her," he said. "In a way I did love her, but once the business was on its feet, I just lost interest."
A shock of astonishment washed through me. "You mean you married her for her money?"
"No, that's oversimplifying. It was a partnership and it had a purpose. *Yes* there was her father's money, but don't forget we started what's now become one of the most important computer businesses in Africa. It wasn't personal

greed or selfishness."

"I see. And the two of you have been together ever since?"

"On and off," said Mandy. "I was with someone else, and he was married again for a while—well, three times altogether. We always seem to find our way back to one another in the end, don't we love?"

She looked up at him at the end with a quick smile. Till then, as she spoke, she had been watching her fingernail scratch determinedly at an old blob of paint on the porch table, as though that table belonged to her.

"But you haven't married one another?"

"Naow!" drawled Nigel, very English. "I think marriage simply *destroys* relationships."

As on that evening when I first met them, two and a half decades before, now again I wondered what it was that attracted me to these people.

"Did you ever climb Kilimanjaro?" I asked Mandy.

"Please, not this story!" said Nigel. He got up and walked away, under the huge arbutus tree, which in the warmth of the mid-summer evening crackled continuously with dropping bark.

"I did climb it," Mandy said, and looked down. I could see that old beauty in her face, from before.

"But?"

"Well, there was an unpleasant experience."

I told you so! I wanted to shout it, and shake her by the shoulders. *Why the hell didn't you listen to me when I warned you?*

Mandy's eyes were still downcast. Twenty five years. Some things don't heal. I felt a wave of compassion; I couldn't be angry with her.

"It was on the way back, actually. I climbed the mountain, that was no problem—it was glorious, really—well *you* know. But, on the way back," she hesitated, then went on. "It was very *hot,* and I decided to swim."

"Where?"

"In the river."

"*What!*"

"I know. It was foolish. The bilharzia danger alone."

"What happened."

"I put my clothes in a pile on the bank, and jumped into this muddy pool. I swam about for a bit, and when I looked up, there was this Maasai fellow standing beside my clothes, with his spear."

"You had nothing on?"

"No. So I waited, and swam around, but he stayed where he was. I waved at him with my hand to go away. I shouted *'kwenda,'* but he took no notice. I thought the only thing to do was try and reach my jeans. I got out, and ran at him. We had a bit of a tugging match with my jeans, but I got my knife, and managed to stab him, and got my clothes, and got away."

"He didn't use his spear?"

"I can't remember, really. I just remember going for him with the knife, and hitting him, and running. When I got back to Nairobi, I reported it, and the police went down, and tracked him into the bush. They found his body, or what was left of it. They didn't give me any trouble—I mean it was obviously self-defence, nobody questioned that. But still, it is a very *strange* feeling to know that you've been responsible for the ending of someone's life."

I tried to imagine that scene. The man coming upon this surprising sight, a young *mzungu* woman, alone and naked in the river. He watches. Was he aroused? She shouts at him in Swahili which he doesn't understand. Next thing she's running at him, grabbing at her clothes. He resists.

"Where was your wallet?" I asked.

"In my jeans."

"Anything in it?"

"Several hundred shillings."

"He hadn't taken that?"

"No, he was . . . just standing there. Hadn't touched my clothes. I don't know where his cows were. But they told me later he was herding cattle."

"But he had a spear? A Maasai who's killed lions with his weapon! And you got him first with a small sheath knife."

"Surprising, isn't it."

"To say the least."

I wanted to carry on questioning her, get her to describe the scene again in more detail. *Was* he in fact aroused? Did he give any overt sign of aggression? Did he say anything, make any sound at all? I realized it was no good asking her. The only other witness to the events was dead.

After they had left that night, I poured myself a shot of brandy, and sat out under the arbutus watching the reflections in the mirror surface of the Trincomalee Channel, and listening to the steady throb of motors, marine traffic that never stops and is more noticeable in those quiet islands at night. I thought how sad a thing it is that in the world people live at the expense of others, using them to get ahead, or killing them for their own security. It came to me suddenly what the attraction of those people had been for me, since that first day in Pompeii: I thought that they were urbane and beautiful, but that was not it. For someone who had grown up in a simple world in Africa, where the main things to fear were snakes, typhoid, and sunstroke, they had had a sinister fascination: they were the first truly evil human beings I had come across, the first who thought of nothing but their own self-interest. They satisfied their own desires, reckless of what damage they might leave behind them.

When I told this to Wilma Vance, she said I was being melodramatic. "Those people aren't *evil!*" she said. "That's not real evil, that's carelessness, like the people in *Gatsby.*"

"Well," I said, "I'll agree to differ with you on that."

One thing I know is this: if some day, in Australia, or Copenhagen, or on a street in Buenos Aires, I hear a voice behind me declaiming a set piece in articulate Latin, I shall not stop. I shall not answer back.

DEALING LIKE STEEL

My father was dismayed and angry when my first marriage fell apart. He wrote letters from Africa, and we spoke once on the telephone. "I cannot understand how you can put yourself in a position in which people can criticize you," he wrote, "and you don't even *try* to defend yourself!" The arrival of each of his letters distanced him more and more from me. He didn't seem concerned at all about my feelings, or what was going on with me—just his own disillusionment and what people thought. So I turned my back on all that, and set about looking after my own survival.

I rented a tiny house in Deep Cove, originally a primitive summer cabin, now modernized with full services and a fireplace. Those were shade and firelight days, when a new intimate relationship might last only through the playing of two sides of a record. I used to sit on the thick wool rug in front of the fireplace made of boulders, with cats purring at their stations around the room, listening to a song:

Why must you always try to make me over?
Take me as I am or let me be.

I was licking my wounds, and it seemed a good idea to me at the time to accept people as they were and not impose judgments on them. I was trying to relate to people again in gentler ways.

All I really want to do
Is baby be friends with you.

This new mood didn't last long. Soon the missionary force was back, tearing down other people's values through a long night, with a couple of bottles of wine. "Look, Gordon," I said, about the tenth time he brought his guitar to my house and reiterated his dreams of freedom through music, "you're never going to make money at this. Your voice is a mumble. Even the fanciest audio equipment isn't going to enhance it enough to get you a record contract. You're kidding yourself, man! Go play guitar in a band. That you *can* do. I like the songs, you know. They're delicate and true. But they won't make money. And you can't sing. Go downtown to 'The Classical Joint' and offer to sing for free. See if anyone'll listen. You're wasting your time coming over here, playing for me and the cats. The freedom you're after is the kind that money buys. Get a well-paying job like your brother, save like crazy for a couple of years, and then you can take time off to sit around writing songs. When the money runs out, go back and do it all over again. Till you get tired of it, and find out what you really want. Then do that."

"Shit, you bastard!" he said. "I come to your house with a bottle of wine, and sing you my songs—you can't even appreciate it! You tell me to go join my brother driving truck!"

He left and did not return. For me, it was time to get out of the Cove. Gordon's slow strumming around my fireplace, and the daily reflection of candle flames in red wine glasses had made me suddenly wish for a place with brighter light.

The next day, parking my car on Dunbar, I bumped into an old friend, Marcel. Hadn't seen him in years! I grasped his hand and, in a fit of emotion, hugged him.

"Too much!" he said. "You live around here now?"

"I'm moving, somewhere. Where are you now?"

"I've got a studio, right here!" he pointed behind him, and I saw a narrow staircase between two storefronts. "Come on up and look."

I went up to his sparse loft. There was an open kitchen, a sleeping bench with a mattress on it, and easels occupying the main free area under a couple of windows.

"Chess?" he asked.

"Sure."

Marcel brought out a carved wooden chess set, and we began to play—not some fusty intellectual game in a silent study, but a rapid, bullying kind of chess at the kitchen table, with the radio full on. Marcel would pick up his piece and crack it down across the board. "Uh-huh!" he'd say. "Let's see what you're going to do about that!" His energy rekindled my interest, and we played often that year. The excitement of the game began to infect our conversations.

"The imagination is the key," said Marcel cutting the air emphatically with his hand. "We poets and painters have got to rip apart the covers, and expose reality to the dumb damn world that doesn't *want* to understand!" He glared at me in distant anger as though I were part of an imagined collusion. I had read his poems, and couldn't make them out. His paintings were so abstract they looked like gigantic, coloured illustrations for a geometry text. "They *haven't* read Blake!" Marcel insisted. "They haven't understood a *damned thing!*"

His passion was refreshing, but it was hard to get him to spell out the details. He waved his arms around as he spoke, and looked extremely fierce.

His wife had grown tired of all this. She got her lawyer to put the house up for sale, and had taken off with the children to Toronto. Her LSAT scores were in the ninety-third percentile, her transcript from the U of T Law School a string of straight A's. On Articling Day the hottest civil litigation firms in town began calling her at nine a.m. She was admitted to the bar, and attained a proud self-confidence, fat earnings, and praise, from her parents and friends, her colleagues and feminist sisters, and her babysitter. A litigation lawyer, by God!

Marcel couldn't care less. He had imagination and style. Beautiful young women jostled one another to get his attention, and the fact that the older women shook their heads in disgust only sweetened it—they were jealous, the bitches.

So, on a particular evening, Marcel brings the wine, and I buy the steak, and we lie back on the comfortable sofas in my new hi-rise apartment while he starts to tell me stories that get my juices running. He's sitting in a pub with Melissa and her girlfriends. He's never taken a good look at Melissa before, knows her only slightly. Now his eyes wander over her body, and he looks right through the clothes. He wants her.

"Let's go!" he says.

"Can't!" she says. "I have to drive my friends home."

Marcel sees her car keys sitting on the table between beer glasses. He reaches out and takes them, and tosses them to one of the friends, who reacts fast and catches them.

"Drive yourselves home in Melissa's car," he says, and stands up.

Melissa follows him out of the pub, and while he drives up the hill to Dunbar Heights, with the tachometer red-lining, she begins running her fingers up and down the seam of his jeans. In his studio, they rip their clothes off and throw the mattress on the floor. "Sixty-nineing like crazy for a good hour!" says Marcel. When they have exhausted one another, they finally subside into a deep well of sleep.

She wakes up refreshed, and wakes him with kisses. She fetches the Chivas Regal bottle, swirls a mouthful of it on him, and they go at it again. She clamps her thighs around his face till he can feel her throb on his tongue. All the next morning they sleep, then eat a lunch of cheese and wine, in the nude. They spend the afternoon stroking and massaging and cupping and sliding and licking and sucking. He is glad to drop her off at her place. He would like to sleep for a while, and then find someone to talk to.

The following night, Marcel is sitting in a bar at closing time, and a stranger comes up to him and smiles. Twenty or so, blonde hair, scents of musk and exotic oil. "Give me a ride home," she says. They drive and park, and walk in through some woods, to where her tiny cabin sits beside a stream.

"It was *just extraordinary!*" says Marcel, curling his tongue around the words. "Who could believe that such a place exists in Burnaby, without even a driveway?"

Her name is Janine. She makes muffins at one a.m. They drink tea with the muffins, and she asks him to stay the night. They get undressed and lie in her bed talking about mountains. He tells her he's a poet and painter. She promises to come over next day to look at some of his work. If not next day, some time soon.

In the following week, Marcel sleeps with three different women. When Janine comes round to see his paintings and poems, he is lying on the mattress in the studio with Mary. After initial awkwardness, they all have coffee together, then Mary leaves. Janine takes off her clothes, and she and Marcel spend the rest of the day on the mattress, talking about mountains and stroking one another. Janine has unbelievably beautiful breasts, but her ass is no good—it simply doesn't turn Marcel on. Still, he loves to fondle and look at her breasts, so what the hell. They look at a couple of paintings, and she tells him she wishes she had a more developed visual sense. Marcel takes another look at her ass, but no, really, it does nothing for him. He doesn't offer to show her any poems, and she doesn't ask. After she leaves, he calls Adrienne, but there's no answer. He calls Michelle, and her phone is busy. He waits. It's still busy.

"Fuck it!" says Marcel, and drives down to the bar, but changes his mind and heads for Melissa's. Melissa has her period, and doesn't feel like taking off her pants. They lie on the carpet of her apartment watching *Masterpiece Theatre,* and she ends up giving him a blowjob. She doesn't particularly want Marcel to sleep the night with her, but if he wants to he can. *Noblesse oblige!* Marcel kisses her gently, kisses her gallantly on both cheeks, kisses her again, bids her a fond goodnight and drives home. He drinks up what's left of the Chivas Regal.

He calls Adrienne. After the fourth ring she answers sleepily, and Marcel suddenly realizes it's 1:30 in the morning.

"Oohh!" he coos, "you *poor* baby! I didn't realize how late it was. I'm so sorry! End of conversation, or . . . ? And just when I really wanted to come round and be with you. I'm such an inconsiderate bastard."

"No," she says sleepily. "It's all right. I understand."

"Oh that's good. Well, what do you think? Not too late for you? Shall I come over?"

She hesitates a second, then says perhaps better not. Marcel urges the idea. She's silent, then confesses in a low voice, "I do want to see you . . . ."

Marcel stirs with excitement. Women! Aren't they just wonderful? But then her voice continues in the barest of soft, enticing whispers:

"But tonight is . . . well it would be crowded."

Marcel apologises at once, and puts down the phone. "Bitch!" he cries. "Some guy in bed with her, and she teases me on!" He stares at the empty Chivas Regal bottle, glares at it, picks it up by the neck and smashes it on the counter.

There is glass all over the floor. Marcel doesn't care. "I am not bloody well going to bed now!" he yells.

He searches the wall for Mary's number, and calls her, listens to it ring, ring, ring. No answer! He is so angry now, he dials Michelle's number again in a fit of masochism. "What a shitty world we live in! Just a pile of fucking crapola!"

But Michelle answers on the second ring. "Marcel, sweetie!" she cries in unabashed delight. "Where *were* you, I *called* you earlier? I had a party on the spur of the moment and couldn't reach you. Everyone's going home, but can't you come around? I really want to *see* you!"

Marcel takes a shower, makes it to Michelle's by 2:30. She's sitting up waiting for him by candlelight, in a silky red robe, with a bottle of Asti and some asparagus vinaigrette. She has cleared up the party, and taken a shower, and her house is fresh and tranquil. They talk quietly on the gravelly bottom registers of their voices, while they swallow and sip, and their eyes are big and round and glistening in the candlelight. They make love with slow, sensual movements on the top of Michelle's bed, then wrap their arms around one another under the covers, and pass into oblivion. Marcel makes it to work next morning at the Emily Carr College of Art and Design, and calls me after his first lecture, and tells me he wants to have dinner tonight, and if I cook the steak, he's bringing the wine.

So Marcel and I sit around after dinner, drinking, while he tells me about his sex life, every sensual and aesthetic detail, and—most important—which one sleeps most comfortably. I keep getting the descriptions switched around.

"But she sucks like—"

"Are you kidding! It's her tongue."

"I thought that was Melissa."

"No!"

I look at him, and here it comes, I can feel it happening: "Marcel," I say, "when did you last do some work?"

He looks at me in surprise. "I was at work today!"

"Not *teaching*, Marcel! Your painting. When did you last write a poem?"

He lights the fifteenth cigarette, frowning, contemplates, sighs, blows out the smoke through his nose. "You can't force it," he says. "When it's time for it to happen it'll happen."

"Sure," I say, "as long as there's no breasts or bums or

mouths in the way. Christ man, this stuff is all terrific, really terrific, I mean I'm burned up with jealousy just listening to you."

"Aahh, c'mon!" He hurls out a laugh and rubs my head, and pours himself some more wine.

"But listen, man . . . ."

"You're absolutely right!"

He sinks back with his glass, and frowns deeply.

I get up and put a record on.

Why must you always try to make me over?

Take me as I am or leave me be.

"You know," says Marcel, "none of them mean a thing to me. I don't care if I ever see any of them again. They're all stupid. All dumb bitches."

Now he begins to suck down the wine like crazy. He can't get enough of the stuff, carefully pouring each glass and seconds later it's empty. We've gone through both his bottles, and are into a third which I took the precaution of hiding. There's a fourth one hidden somewhere else, and I suppose we'll kill that too before the night ends.

It's not yet midnight, and Marcel's out of cigarettes. I offer him a pipe, but he won't smoke a pipe: "I tried it once, it just makes my mouth feel dirty."

"We need music," Marcel says. "What ever happened to that guy who used to come around in Deep Cove and play the guitar and sing in that terrible snuffling voice?"

"I told him he was wasting his time, and haven't seen him since."

Marcel goes out in search of a cigarette machine, leaving me to confront my emptiness. Christ, I want to fulfil my own ambitions, so I tell this kid who's trying to write songs that he's got no voice. Marcel has a string of beautiful women waiting for his call—they walk up to him in bars and pick him up—he has more trouble finding cigarettes than a supply of gorgeous bodies—so in my jealousy I tell him he should give up sex for painting. Marcel returns, with cigarettes from a machine he has found.

68

"Where are you going to sleep tonight?" I ask.

He looks at his watch. "It's a bit late," he says, reaching nevertheless for the address book in his slim briefcase. "No, no, it's too late! And in any case you're right, I must get centred and start producing again."

"Here." I reach for the book and open it. Marcel goes to my desk and slides a sheet of paper into the typewriter. While he types, I flip through the indexed pages.

"What is it you want from women, Marcel?"

No answer. Just the tapping of the typewriter keys.

"I think you may be looking for the wrong thing," I say. "That's why you end up calling them bitches."

Tap tap tap, te-dap tap tap, te-dap tap "Shut up," says Marcel.

He rips paper from the machine and scrunches it into balls which he throws into the corner of the room. "More wine!" he calls.

I get up and fetch the second of the hidden bottles, and open it. He grabs it out of my hand while I'm pouring, and swigs down mouthfuls like a thirsty pirate. "Ah yes!"

He's bashing away on the machine, and his new pack of cigarettes is beginning to look crumpled and empty.

He finishes his poem, rips it out of the typewriter, and reads it to me with dramatic enunciation, conducting the tempo of the syllables with his right hand. It's something about the princess and the frog. No new visions of reality, just Marcel dressing up his sexual adventures in literary posturing.

"Good!" I say.

"It's no damn good at all," Marcel spits, "but at least it's a start. What time is it?"

"It's 1:15."

"Damn! Too late! I can't go phoning people again in the middle of the night."

I open his book and start reading names. Sylvia, Charlotte, Deena, Marilyn—"

"Marilyn!" He smiles like a fish leaping. He reaches for

69

the book, lights a cigarette, takes a swig from the wine bottle, lifts the phone and puts it down again. "No, it's too late," he says.

"Here." I take the book and dial the number. "Marilyn?" I say. "Listen, you don't know me but I'm here with my friend Marcel, and he thinks it's too late to be calling you . . . ."

Marcel drives off to spend the night with Marilyn. In the towel drawer I have hidden the real emergency reserve, the third extra bottle, and I open it. Across the mouth of the inlet and up the mountain, the chairlift lights burn on.

Marcel will not get himself centred just yet, I think, but *I sure wish* I had a little of his appetite for himself, instead of this perpetual urge to go making other people over, not admitting my own desires, my own failures.

Three months ago, it was, he drove away from my apartment in the middle of the night. No word from him since.

What is this extraordinary compulsion, to enter other people's lives and tell them what they should be doing? At times like this I wish my father were still alive to talk to. *Tell me, Father, where did this come from? When did it begin, and when is it good or bad? Dealing like steel with people: does it really help them? And what is it doing to me?*

For the past two weeks I have been visiting back East. I see my old friend Nathan in Brockport, N.Y. He shows me the proposal he has written up for his dissertation. I read it and take it apart. I tell him he hasn't thought out clearly what it is he wants to investigate. He says he's trying to find out what teachers think their professional training should consist of, but his language keeps twisting, and it soon appears that he has his own ideas about how they should be trained.

"Nathan, what are you trying to do? Are you trying to assemble an accurate picture of what the teachers think? Or are you trying to tell them what *you* think?"

I spend two hours in his comfortable office, going over

his confusions line by line. Exhausted, humble, he thanks me.

The next day, well-fed and rested, stroked by discussion with his wife, he smiles at me with a loony glower: "Well *that* was quite a session!" he bellows. "It was like going to *the dentist!*" Should I just have left him and accepted what he had done, as I accept Marcel's stories of women?

And last night . . . here I am staying with my old friend Jed and his wife in New Hampshire. The main reason I've come is to celebrate the fact that Jed and his second wife Emily are back together. *My* second wife and I are not back together, but Jed and Emily, by God, have pulled it off.

After we drink the champagne I have brought, Jed shows me the brochure he has printed and addressed and is set to mail out to five hundred people. He wants to start a new magazine, for environmental action.

"It's preaching to the converted," I say. "It's no good. You haven't targeted your audience accurately."

"No good?" he says. "Do you have any idea how many times I've written and rewritten it? Changed it here to accommodate this Board member; changed it there for that Board member. Where do you get off telling me it's no good when I've busted my ass on the damn thing? It's the best I can do, you bastard!"

I begin with the first sentence, and show him what I think is wrong. It takes three hours, and most of a gallon jug of wine. This morning, he thanks me, and goes off to his office to trash the first printing, and do the damn thing over again and mail it out to the five hundred people.

"Thanks!" he says. "I really don't get enough of this kind of criticism."

But his eyes are like the barrels of a shotgun, and I get the feeling he would like to pull the triggers.

Couldn't I have left well enough alone? Instead, I go out and buy porterhouse steak, and cook dinner, and then tell him his brochure was full of errors, and then, when Emily had gone to bed, take the rest of his life apart too, tell him he's in a mess, should never have quit his teaching job three years ago, tell him he should get out of this town and go where he could have a job with a steady cash flow, out of this country in fact, emigrate to Canada and quit trying to buck the Amerikan *Reich?* Where do I get off trying to make Jed over like that, when he's pulled his second marriage back together and is starting a new magazine?

Speak to me, Father.

Marcel (I know it) is awaiting my return home to Vancouver. Can't wait to tell me about a new pair of breasts, an extraordinary ass. It's my role. I'll listen, and then I'll say, "No, Marcel, no! You're looking for the wrong thing again. You're just going to end up calling them bitches."

Marcel will look at me dead serious, and say, "You're right. You're absolutely right! You bastard!"

Next day, some kid with a novel manuscript: "Well?"

"Interesting," I'll tell him. "But the whole thing has to be redone."

I look around in desperation. My father is dead, so there's no use pretending to talk to him. I go to Jed's bookshelf, and eventually settle on Bertrand Russell. I open Volume I of the *Autobiography,* and look at the frontispiece portrait, the set mouth, the wise eyes. "Okay!" I think, "this is some guy, some *life!*" I turn the page and begin: "Three passions, simple but overwhelmingly strong, have governed my life: the longing for love, and the longing for knowledge, and unbearable pity for the suffering of mankind."

"Well, well!"

I settle myself into the chair for a promising read.

"These passions," the book continues, "like great winds, have blown me hither and thither. . . ."

I put the volume down and say aloud, "Oh, Bertie man! You're screwing it up right in the second sentence!"

Quietly, I let myself out of Jed and Emily's house, and walk through the sepiatone moonlit streets, down to the Merrimack river. I sit on a cold bench, listening to the gurgle of water tumbling through an iron grate. The noises sound like words, garbled and fleeting.

.

BEGINNING THE SPRING

One Saturday night, near the end of my sabbatical year in the Gulf Islands, I got a phone call I had half expected from Claudio, the union treasurer. An important vote, he said: a vote to call a strike vote. First time in the history of Canyon College.

"I think you should be there," he said. "You're needed, buddy."

We were bored, Victor our neighbour, Jessica and me. I had finished writing my textbook, Jessica was taking a break before finding another band to sing with, and Victor was trying to dream up a way of making a living. The cold days of March had dragged on into an empty April. Even the fishing was no longer interesting. We sat around the fire talking about our future plans, our future lives, all of us discontented—tired of one another's boredom and our own— on that beautiful island, smoking late, watching the fire burn out, adding here a brick, there a wall to these fantasy future lives of ours, and listening to music.

But getting that phone call had rekindled some excitement in me.

"Damn it, what will I use for a car?" Mine was being fixed in Victoria, major engine damage—but that's another story.

"Take the truck," said Vic, and tossed me the keys to his ancient Fargo.

Vic left very late that night, and Jessica and I went to bed too tired for even basic sex. So when the alarm went off for me to catch the early ferry—the only ferry—it was as though I hadn't slept, as though the record was still playing. The music had persisted, like an electromagnet that has put certain lines of force into me, and in the morning I still have them. So I lift the body, not even enough sleep to get hung-over, thinking if I don't get to the road by 6:15—and it's probably icy too—then that's it, because they don't wait on that early run, and I find, automatically, I'm singing.

In Vic's truck (dah; dah; DAH; dah-di-da-dah) trying to fit the key into the ignition ("that poo-oor gir-rl / tossed by the tides of MIS-fortune") and finally getting it in ("in the quiet morning, la dah-dah-dah-DAH etc.) and it turns . . . nothing!

The whole build-up for nothing. Dead battery, whatever. I sure ain't gonna make that ferry, as my friend Marcel would put it. (Janis Joplin gone . . . the romance of it, the music winding down to the funeral in my head.) You understand about people getting out of stalled cars on freeways and kicking their wheels. Damn it, I won't even see Marcel! Might as well go back to bed and build up the hangover with a second round of sleep.

Hah! A whine, a drone, a CAR! Shit, somebody else from East Point going to catch the 6:40? And where is it coming from? In this quiet, you learn to recognize the sound of individual cars, like a dog, and I don't recognize this one. It doesn't even seem to be up on the road; what direction is it coming from?

Aphrodite *anadyomene,* rising out of the ocean—it's a surprise of that order to me, the solitary observer. Off our beach (how long has it been there, what did they steal?), an orange Sport-Yak raft on the roof, comes this Land Rover with three people in it, and drives across my astonished gaze, over the field, up to the driveway, and behind the trees. The day is saved, hooray. (A *vehicle* came off our *beach!*)

Wait! I forgot to stop them.

I plunge upwards over the seeded fall, drowning my city shoes in mud, and get to East Point Road before they pass, wave, and they stop.

I instantly dislike them. Terrible people—except for the fact that they have stopped to give me a ride. I have been driven along this narrow road by drunks in unsafe cars, and once by an old man without a driver's licence whose conviction of emergency carried him over the corners, but I have never felt as bad as this. What's the matter with them? Do they resent having to help me, when they themselves are strangers here (doing what, exactly, government crest on the door?) and having me breathe whisky over them, and my chatter. I hate them. Maybe they haven't woken up yet. Or is it a triangle? There are two men, one about forty, one about twenty five, and a woman in her late twenties. Why are they emanating bad vibes at six fifteen on a bright morning in the islands? Where did they sleep?

"Come over last night?"

"mnnmnnyerr."

"You're not going to Vancouver, are you?"

"mmnnarr rrrnnggyaaarr rrictorrrrierrr."

"Oh! So you must be the survey team, come out to look at Tumbo for a provincial park?" (Who told me this last night, Victor, Jessica, or did I actually *dream* in that short time?)

Silence. Ditto. Ditto.

They don't want to answer, so fuck 'em. They come over here on *my* tax money, sleep on *my* beach, drive across *my* field (well, rented) and make decisions about *my* environment, and they don't even have the manners to talk to me. Gggo bagg to rrictorrrrierrr where you belong, assholes!

On the little ferry, I get right away from them and drink my tea without bothering to take note of what they're doing, whether dribbling words to one another, or slimy snake looks, snickering with their disgusting lips that I'm still drunk from the night before. Fuck em! Unimportant human trash—what we have to put up with—what governs our lives in this abundant and over-regulated country. Unemotional, unimaginative, unmannered. Civil serpents.

Easy now. Why all this hostility (in the quiet morning)? Janis Joplin's been dead quite a while, and in any case you don't even like her singing—gave away *Pearl* because you couldn't stand her ego strutting its twist over other people's songs. All right, easy then, sip, sip the tea.

But it continues with me. Was it the whisky breath, or was it because of who had been sleeping with whom on which seat of the Land Rover, or a nylon pup tent that flounced and beat in the night? Or, for God's sake, did one of them get left behind on our beach while the other two rode out to Tumbo in the Sport-Yak II after supper, to fumble one another on the freezing oyster rocks, getting cut . . . well, and so on. I glance over in contempt at her, to see what she looks like anyway. Ugly.

I am standing on the car deck, looking at them all sitting there in their warm little selfish seats, smugly waiting to drive off. Bastards. Listen, when I sit where you are now sitting, and I see some person obviously wandering about between the lanes while the boat docks, I open my door on the passenger side and lean out and yell, "Hey, you wanna ride?" And give it to them, perhaps going a few kilometres out of my way if necessary.

Oh I hate them. I will not stoop to ask a single one of them for a ride. I will not even go to the rusty red pickup and say, "Hey man, do you mind if I ride in the back to the freeway or wherever?"

Determined, I walk three kilometres down the causeway. I remember the last time I walked it, at eleven o'clock one night, after coming off the late ferry, and my car was in the parking lot, but I'd gone and left the lights on for five days, and the B. C. Ferries truck was away for servicing, and the guy said, "Ask the Highways Department guy," which I did, and he looked at his watch and drawled slowly, "We-ell, I guess I just went off duty," and so help me, smiled, and started his truck (*my* truck, *my* tax money), and drove away. So, after walking the three clicks now, I break down and put out my thumb.

Big heavy Oldsmobile, about 1957, cautiously kept, not a sign of rust, not a spot on the seats. "Very kind of you," I say, getting in. "Are you heading for Vancouver by any chance?" and he says, "Ja."

He talks about the weather. I tell him I'm coming in to a union meeting. For fifteen minutes then, all the way to the Oak Street bridge, he delivers a poisonous, whinging tirade on workers and wage settlements (making a mockery of democracy and killing the little man, putting him out of business).

"Yeah, well," I say, as his voice rises emotionally. The sun is coming through the windshield good and warm. He—what! I look again, yes—he starts to cry. Not a muscle, not a flicker, not even a sniff, just these old cloudy tears sliding down in the skin furrows beside his nose and making a dry pfft! on his pants, punctuated by "I hef bin union member! I hef *been* union member!" pfft pfft, and the tears make wet patches on the dry material till he's starting to look like a pissed rubby.

"Well God dammit I'm sorry if you're being squeezed out of your living, man, but I've got to fight for my rights! That's all."

Silence. The old car yaws and pitches on shocks that have lost it. The morning is so fresh and bright! The tea and toast in my stomach are turning acid.

"You know . . . ." He starts about the war. Broken families, dead children, a building gone just like that (his hand cuts the air so fast I can hear it), then: "I was fighting, you know, I was . . . member of the army . . . and we were parachuting into a certain country, five of us dere were, und zey shot us, you know, from de ground, Russian soldiers with rifles, you know, from de ground, hanging in our parachutes."

"They hit you?"

"Four dead. Me only is living."

"God."

I stare at the bulrushes at the side of the freeway, the frost on the brown cattails, thinking: "What does he do, drive out to Tsawwassen every time the urge comes on him? And picks up hitchhikers and tells them this story (holds them with his glittering eye)? And then goes home to Surrey or Richmond and changes pants, and drives down to some little store in Steveston or Ladner where the union bullies are putting the squeeze on him. And sits, remembering?"

By now, it's eleven o'clock. I'm back on the sidewalk at 25th and Cambie, where the lawns are all tidy, and the houses on one side of the boulevard have even newer roofs than those on the other. A huge black Ford pulls up. The ashtray is overflowing with butts, and as we pull away empty beer bottles, brown stubbies, roll against each other on the floor at the back. A young, hefty guy with a bad face. He stinks of booze and smoke. I listen to the Country Western singer on the radio: "Well I start out the evenin' bein' selective / Take what I can get by two. / I never went to bed with an ugly woman / But I sure woke up with a few." His driving is a series of lurchings and brake stabs. I noticed the front and back ends had bits of metal hanging off them, from careless parking.

"Well how ya doing?" I yell above the radio.

"Bad."

"How's that?"

"Why does a person always lose their friends?"

He says he's been driving around since it happened, trying to figure it out. He says this isn't the first time either.

Broke a bottle and shoved it into his best buddy's face.

"Beer bottle?"

"Yeah."

"Christ, you cut him?"

"Look here. Blood all over." He holds his arm up. Three dried lines of blood curve down from the wrist to the elbow.

"Well, Jesus, is he all right?"

"I dunno. I left when they called the cops."

And he's been driving around since, trying to figure it out. Why does a person always lose their friends? I tell him it's the bottles. Yeah, but why does he *do* the bottle thing? Is it always the same, then?

"Sure. The last one, Rick, he had to have forty-three stitches in his face and he can't breathe proper."

It isn't the thought that if I took long enough and drove around all day with him in this hot car I'd get to the bottom of it with him. That doesn't interest me—because getting to the bottom of it is just getting to the beginning of this particular story, and it will not end. It's the thought of this guy every so often doing this. And others. Just driving around the city streets, trying to figure stuff like this out. He lets me off on Hastings, shakes his head, says sure, shakes his head, he's gone.

On the bus, two elderly women behind me converse. One speaks volumes, and the other has a telegraphic style. Each volume begins at a point, and goes through nine different themes before returning to that point, and then there's a pause. Then comes the telegram. Then the beginning of volume two. They seem to belong in a retirement home, but that can't quite be it. Now they're talking about the cost of food.

". . . and you know the other day I slipped into Woodward's just quickly you know because if you don't get that 3:15 it's impossible and he won't tell them to move back, or he tries, but his voice is so weak and anyway half the time they're liquored up and he's so young, and I slipped in for a couple of nice pork chops, well first you can't find them they cut them so thin nowadays fast fry they call it because of all these young people living in apartments, which is a shame really I feel so sorry for the young things trying to make a go of it today and the cost of houses being out of all proportion, and some green peppers and maybe a bit of bread because I wasn't sure the old loaf was still good, you know I buy that Bio bread with the good texture because you need that, you know the roughage, and of course but they don't put preservatives in any more and so naturally it goes off, or at least *I* think it does, and maybe yes I think it was a litre, no two litres of the two percent though honestly I don't see what harm it does to drink the homo but who wants to argue with the doctor when you're in their hands, and of course you have to wait in line so long now, and I knew there wasn't a chance in the world, I'd have to wait for the 3:30, and it was seven dollars, seven dollars, I just couldn't believe it!"

Silence.

Then the other says: "I never shop at Woodward's."

"Well of course a person has their own individual likes and dislikes, I never go into that awful butcher's anymore not since they got horse meat in the front case . . ." (etcetera) ending, "Why not?"

And the other, finally dragged out by the silence says, "I just don't."

"What's your reason?"

Suddenly it's become exciting. Confrontation politics, short and unavoidable.

"No reason."

Again, the voluble one launches into tolerant statements about freedom of choice, but finally her mind will not let the matter go fuzzy. "A person has a reason," she says. "There's always a reason, a person has to have a reason for what they do. Don't they?"

There's a long, charged silence. Then the telegraph voice

gathers strength and courage from remote provinces, I can feel it behind me like electric potential (even as the other voice repeats like dah; dah; dah; dah-di-da-DAH, the dying chorus of a song: "A person has to have a reason!"), and she says, "But they don't have to tell it."

They don't have to tell it!

I can hear breathing. Dry, bitter flames lick the air, curling against one another, blue flame against red flame, and silence. There has been an alteration of balance. This will take some time to settle, quite some time. It will have to be paid for, assessed and paid for, in the proper currency. I turn to look at them, my head an irreverent intrusion between their two battling faces.

When I get off to change buses, the thing is so polarized it does not come away with me. It sticks fast in the Hastings bus, and is carried east into Burnaby. I forget it quickly, like smashed glass, swept and gone.

In the late morning of the clear, bright, warming spring day, the tannic acid has mollified. I'm hungry for soft meat, potatoes and gravy, a nice easy beer. A good lunch before the meeting anyway. I get on the last bus for the last short leg, and it's almost empty. Five or six people, and the fresh breeze blowing in the windows. The driver is youthful, and whistling. Opposite me, a man smiles, and my response is instantaneous:

"Is that gold? That's beautiful."

He has on a gold chain round his neck, an Olympic coin, a hundred-dollar gold piece. He has given up driving, he says, and is turning his gas savings into gold. This is the first hundred. It shines, oh how it shines in the brilliant spring day. His clothes are matched and tasteful; he wears them with satisfaction. He's young, but his hair is thinning. He has a vulnerable smile, like one who has suffered. His manners seem gentle.

I like gay men. I almost invariably find them witty and full of good sense and charming manners. I reach out to finger his coin delicately, and compliment him on it more couthly now than before (duh). He makes me feel like a bumpkin. We talk about the body's need for exercise. I tell him about the man who gave me a ride in from Tsawwassen, shot at as he dangled in the air. German— Czech—Hungarian—I couldn't really tell which side he fought on in the war.

"Hungarian," he says confidently, he knows them well.

"How's that?"

"If you ever played soccer against Hungarians, you'd know. They're mean and sneaky. They snitch all the time to the referee, but when they cheat or foul, oh no, that's a different story!"

I look around the bus. This is the worst shock of the day. I stare into the man's face. Everybody is watching. Everybody has heard.

And all I can manage is a mumble: " But . . . merrgg nyerrm people of different cultural backgrounds have different ways, what one culture abhors another may consider normal."

"Normal? Huh! They shouldn't let them play soccer. Heave them out of the league. I hate Hungarians!"

I am speechless. When does this ride end?

"But the worst," he continues, "the very WORST, are the ITALIAN PLAYERS! I would rather not play soccer at all than have to play with the Italians. NAH!"

I whirl my head. Everybody is watching me. And then the bus stops, and everybody gets off, and I have still not been able to act. Somebody needs to shoot somebody. Ground glass in the wounds. We need to wrap our enemies in parachute silk and bury them. God, but the world is strange today. To get up in another world, with melodic dirge lines magnetizing your brain still "in the quiet morning," and ride, and ride in *("in on a sea of disaster, rode out on a mainline trail").* . . .

At the union meeting, attendance is high and the mood

is grim. We have never been on strike before, and people are nervous. We have not saved. We are academics, with little practical experience of these matters. Some of us have experience, or at least clear instincts, but others are confused. The union is divided. "Let's be *reasonable!*" says one of the natural scientists. "All I want to know," one member calls out in a morally correct voice, "is *are* we going on strike or *aren't* we?" The strategists stare at him wearily.

For two solid hours I listen to motions and countermotions. Money is not the issue. Benefits are not the issue. Is there a strikeable issue or isn't there? It's the part-timers. They must get access to the same salary scale and benefits as everybody else. The College is offering them access after ten years. Scandalous! They must get access after two years, or at most three. They must not be treated as second-class citizens. Most of them are women, and some single parents. They need the money, and the benefits. Everything else can go. On this we stick. Why not let this go too, somebody suggests. Why not poll the members and find out, as management proposed?

It changes then. The tone of the language suddenly hardens. The middle ground has gone.

A wave of emotion puts me on my feet. "Listen here," I say. My foot goes up on the chair to keep me steady. I feel a surge of anger forcing up inside me, and I don't want to get out of control. "Listen here, that's crap!" I say. "That's a pile of horseshit and you all know it! You want to say I'm all right Jack, and sell out people like Joanne and Marylou? Like hell you do! This union's united and that's all there is to say. Management tells the negotiating team to go poll the membership, and we sit here arguing like idiots whether it should be by show of hands or secret ballot or a mail ballot. It's the same divisive tactic they've been pulling for the last hundred years!"

I lose my temper, and begin shouting out of control. "Every time you've come back to us, we've given you a solid mandate to go back in there and stand firm. So if anybody in this room does not agree, LET THEM SPEAK UP NOW! If anyone is feeling disaffected, LET THEM COME FORWARD NOW!"

Someone starts clapping, but my temper is running on, and I'm shouting and making a total fool of myself. Half my friends are cracking up with laughter, as the words roll on and on from my mouth and my gut, and I can't stop them. The strike vote passes by over eighty percent. I feel stupid and spent. I feel terrific. Claudio comes over with a big smile and takes my hand. "Hey! Man!" he says.

I look at my watch. "You gonna drive me to the ferry?" I ask.

"You got it!" says Claudio.

Back on the island, I catch a ride in the back of Jacksons' pickup, and when they drop me off, I stride down the seeded fall, the music almost gone (in the quiet morning— already the echo dead), and Jessica has dinner laid out, with candles and white wine. I talk nonstop while we eat, and then in bed as we make love.

Eventually, in the silence Jessica says: "You sure had yourself one hell of a day, boy."

"Hey," I say. "It's the beginning of spring."

ESTHER: A SPRING SKETCH

I must get a key cut for her. I'll go down to Jensen's Hardware, talk to the East Indian guy about Kenya, speak with his old father in Swahili. They'll tell me again that butter is now fifty shillings a pound in Nairobi. *From two shillings and twenty-five cents to fifty shillings!* I don't believe it. But they need to say such things, to believe all of Africa is outrageous. Perhaps they had relatives in Uganda. Tortured, or killed. Nobody can live with the simple facts. People have to weave intricate webs of language around horrors so stark. "Anyway, listen," I say, "I just read that President Moi has released all political prisoners. Amnesty International has given Kenya a clean bill of health."

Already, while I'm saying it, his head starts that sideways rocking, childlike noises in his throat. "And you believe it?"

The old man is happy, anyway, to be out of that continent. I ask him for a mousetrap in Swahili, and he smiles and sets off down the aisle to get one. The old man's vacant, contented smile is his wisdom. He leaves the politics to his son.

"And this key."

The son inspects it with a frown, studying the pattern. I explain that sometimes it won't turn, you have to pull it out a bit, so maybe he can adjust the cutting, because I want the new one to work.

"Definitely!"

He wants to talk more, start on Tanzania maybe. I just want the key now, and to get out of here.

"*Kwa heri, Mzee!*" Goodbye, sir.

The old man puts his head to one side, gracefully: "*Haya, kwa heri sasa!*" So, goodbye for now.

Walking home, I wonder if they feel any guilt or regret for having left and immigrated to Canada. Days so vacant in this peaceful country that the word "mousetrap" in the old language puts a smile on their faces.

And I'm a sort of refugee, too.

And Esther too. Running away from fear.

I walk down Broadway, away from Idi Amin, soldiers raping the women in front of their husbands, lifetime savings frozen by Exchange Control. It's all right, they have begun again. A few cents on a mousetrap, a few more on a key. And I am walking into Esther, her presence tonight when she arrives. My house her haven. A room of her own for a few days, till she makes her new start. I have advised her to park down the street in case he decides to come looking for her, and begins checking out the homes of all her friends. Once, he smashed her locked door so violently it lifted the frame right out of the wall. It would not surprise me one bit to have a rock come through my front window. Or a bottle.

Buy daffodils. Buy grapefruit. Walk around the produce stalls and pick out a whole bouquet of fruits. Pears. Three different kinds of imported oranges. A large red apple. And a bunch of black grapes.

She isn't really afraid of him hitting her. She expects it at some point and is resigned. "I don't mind blood," she said. We all know he's likely to do it, and there's no point trying to stop him. It would only provoke him more. Even if we called the police on him, got a restraining order—even if some of us took it on ourselves to try to beat it out of him before he beats her—still he would wait for his opportunity. The only absolute way of preventing his attack would be to kill him.

What I am concerned about is the key. Esther is so depleted that I can see her coming to the door and finding it won't work, and just giving up. I see her helplessly trudging back to her car with an armful of clothes, and getting in and just driving off, anywhere.

I clean the room. Wash the sheets. Lift the glass top off the desk and wipe it on both sides, rubbing up a shine with newspaper. I clear out all my junk and pile it in a closet in my bedroom. The paint is bad, and I wish there was time to do a quick job, yellow or a nice bright cream. I'll give her the key this afternoon at the Press office, but I have to teach late so I won't be here tonight when she comes. Everything must be in order, simple and clean and welcoming.

I wash a large, fluffy towel for her. Already the basket of fruits is filling the room with a mix of scents. The daffodils are fragile and papery in the tall, stone vase. I hope that she'll wake tomorrow morning with a smile. Heart pounding like a child's. I'd like her to open her eyes on bright sunlight streaming into the room. And hear a bird singing in the apple tree. Just that one clear sound in a lull of traffic, and her heart will jump for joy, as we used to say.

Esther deserves all the love and small attentions we can give. When she first came to work for us at the Press, it was soon obvious that something was wrong. She went against all our advice with this man. I told her once, frankly, he was a psychopath, and saw her staring over my shoulder; I turned, and there he was, standing in her kitchen doorway behind me. Marcel couldn't even bring himself to be polite to the man. Once I went to dinner, and bore his drunken putdowns of her all evening long, and went home and dreamed that he fell off a fishboat and drowned.

But for two years she persisted. When she realized that there was no way of getting us to understand what she saw in him, or why she stuck with him, she never once complained. She knew that we were opposed, and made no call on us. When his excesses threw her into awful debts, charge accounts that she simply couldn't pay and a kitchen full of liquor bottles and no food, she would not come to us for loans; she began to sell some of her possessions.

We could make excuses for ourselves. Like those who tolerate a corrupt regime, we could say that we did not know how bad it was, we didn't know what was going on. Oh yes? At *least* subliminally we knew. Strain and humiliation in her face every day—and what did we think when she came in to the Press one morning with a box and began giving away her jewellery? Silver and ivory necklace . . . amber ring . . . .

The fact is we were opposed and would not help her unless she asked. She had made her bed, and it was a bad one, so let her lie in it and find out for herself since she was so stubborn, and wouldn't listen. As though cutting her off would punish her, and bring her to her senses.

Meanwhile, look what she had done for us. When Marcel and his wife split up, Esther took him into the apartment she then had, and charged no rent. Six months of that, feeding him and listening to his pain, and all the while having to fend off her own boyfriend at the time, whom she wanted to marry and who was jealous of all the attention Marcel was getting. And when I needed it, she became my lover. When I pulled away, she uttered no reproach and closed no door. How many times have I gone to her as to an elder sister, confused, and troubled, and usually drunk. How many times have I walked into her place and gone *Phew!* into her arms, her sofa, her bed. Once, I came to sleep with her for comfort, and threw up all over her sheets in the middle of the night, disgusting mess of Greek food and bottle upon bottle of cheap red wine. Marcel can tell his own shabby stories. And other people too. Her grandparents are probably too far gone to realize that she keeps them from being put in a home by her twice- and three-times-a-week visits way across town, to wash their soiled clothes and bedding, and bodies.

She came. There was no problem. She managed the key fine.

I didn't see her till the next day at the Press. She smiled at me, her beautiful, directionless, half-lunatic smile. "You're a very nice man," she said, and I could have wept for the dismal gap between all that she deserves and our little dollar-forty-nine gestures of fruit and flowers.

It was then I realized that it's her lunacy that touches me. She acts sane, and at the same time she's absolutely crazy. She walks about the office and functions efficiently at her job—never makes mistakes, not even a typo. She drives fast and with precision. She buys tasteful clothing, and sews, and sits on the Arts Board. But inside, the whole structure of her life is gone. Her mother is long dead, and she plays out that role to the grandparents. Her father is somewhere else, always fretting over money. Everything collapsed for Esther a long time ago, and there's nothing but a buzzing limbo there. Her only supports are her weekly conversations with her psychiatrist, and her journal writing. Nothing seems to follow logically any more . . . she can't find things where she expected them to be . . . she can't remember three-quarters of what she said or promised to do yesterday. Yet she faces the world with that look of smiling discovery: somehow it's all right, *everything just seems to be all right* . . . . You look into her eyes, and she closes her mouth and smiles at you, and you feel your own heart beat.

She'll stay here. She has a room of her own for a day or a week or as long as she likes. The key fits the lock. The red apple shines darkly in the basket. Traffic, moving constantly on the road outside, appears to soothe her; she told me that she sat and watched it for hours on end. Down the street, the hardware merchant talks about the price of butter in Nairobi. His old father smiles, remembering, *mtego ya panya:* mousetrap.

ROADKILL

It's curious how time will change a story. You live through something with somebody, and twenty or thirty years later you have different versions of it, depending on the people involved.

One weekend in 1958, when I was Master-on-Duty at the Prince of Wales school, Nairobi, a phone call came in from Bobs Harries, the big pineapple farmer at Thika.

"Where's Mr. Fletcher?" the voice demanded. "This is urgent."

"The Headmaster's off-duty now, sir. Can I help you?"

"Well, you'll have to get a lorry," he said. "I've got about a ton of pineapples here that are too ripe to market. You can have them for the boys, but you'll have to come and fetch them. Do you want them? Because if not, I'll give them to St. Mary's."

"We'll take them. Thanks Mr. Harries."

I left the office unattended, and scooted over to Fletcher's house, and volunteered to truck in the pineapples in my Fordson pickup.

"Splendid!" he said. "But now who will mind the phone?"

"That's the problem," I said.

"Oh, very well," said PF. "Go back and switch the phone through to my house, and off you go to Thika."

"Yes sir. But I think it's going to take more than one trip."

PF sighed. "Yes, I expect it is," he said.

I went back to my house and woke my Australian friend Wade, the new math teacher, who had stopped to earn some money on his travels around the world.

"Wanna see a bit of the country?"

"Too right."

So we set off for Thika, a journey of some forty miles—or a hundred and sixty, by the time we had made two return trips. I was whistling happily. I hated those weekend duties. You sat in the sterile office all day, and usually nothing ever happened. I'd get so bored, I'd end up staring out the window, over the playing fields, dreaming up a smoker or some other culprit I could rush out and catch. This was a lot better.

Wade and I hadn't known each other long—two or three weeks, something like that. I found his Australianisms charming, and sometimes funny. We stopped for gas and oil, and when I opened the side bonnet of the Fordson, Wade said, "My! What a dinky little power unit!" Power unit, indeed! What's wrong with calling an engine an engine. (The previous Saturday, when Wade rode out on his Lambretta to my family home at Kiambu, for dinner, he said he'd had no trouble finding the way.

"Only trouble was, the road was chockablock with wogs!"

"Oh."

I didn't know which way to look.

My father cleared his throat.

"Well," my stepmother said diplomatically, "it's the time of day. Shall we eat?"

"I mean I've ridden across Europe, and half the height of Africa, and I've never *seen* so many wogs!" said Wade. "I tell you, I *really* ran into them!"

"Ran into them?" I repeated, incredulous.

"Take a look at m'windscreen, willya?"

I stepped outside with him, father and stepmother gingerly following, to witness some ghastly sight I couldn't quite imagine. Blood and jagged perspex?

"See?"

The Lambretta was caked with dust, and the windshield made almost opaque by the greenish body fluids of smashed grasshoppers and other insects.

"These? You call these 'wogs'?" I said.

"'Sright. Dont*chu?*"

"Well, no. The word has another connotation here."

"When we say wogs, we mean pollywogs, these."

"We prefer the Swahili word, *ndudu*," my Father announced. And for the second time, my stepmother suggested we go and eat.

"Oh!" Wade laughed aloud at her. "You thought I'd run over some *black paiple!* That's what you meant when you said it was the time of day!"

"Yes, people are coming off work, and the road is crowded with bicycles and pedestrians."

Earlier, our house servant, Muthoni, had come to me with a blank look on her face. "Whack us up a shirt wouldya, Merthowny?" Wade had said, and I explained to her that he wanted her to iron for him. He made no concessions of pronunciations or language—other than that one instance, where he took my father's hint and called the insects "doo-doos.")

All the way out to Thika, we chatted away about things I can't remember now. But I still hear the Australian twang, and I know it was that trip that formed the bond between us. We loaded the pineapples, and came swaying back in, dangerously overweight; I was worried, because that stretch of road had the worst accident record in the country, and the police often checked it. We stopped and bought a knife, and began eating pineapples. They were at the peak of ripeness, juicy, and so colourful they actually stained our lips yellow. I drove up to each of the school house dining halls, and we unloaded, then merrily back to Thika again for the second load.

A little while ago as I was making preparations to go back and visit Africa after twenty years I got all excited, and went down to the Vancouver Public Library, and pulled out the phone books for Harare and Bulawayo, Cape Town, Johannesburg—nothing, unfortunately, from Kenya. I copied down addresses into my book, and then suddenly I thought of Wade. I found a New South Wales book—and, wow! There he was. I wrote at once, asking to be excused if it was the wrong guy. But it was him all right. Back came a letter, post haste. All his news of the past thirty years crammed into a couple of pages. I couldn't take it in. And why had I written, anyway? I wasn't going to Australia, I had no chance of seeing him.

A few days later, I reread Wade's letter. Mangoes, he says. "Remember that time we drove out to Thika in your ute and picked up a couple of loads of mangoes for the school? For some reason, that trip is etched forever in my memory."

Why has he changed the pineapples to mangoes? I discuss it at supper with my family.

"Has it occurred to you," says my son, the philosophy major, "that he might be right, and you might be wrong?"

"It's not possible," I said. "Anyone who knows Kenya can tell you, Bobs Harries Estates grew pineapples, not mangoes."

"Anyway," my son says impatiently, "I don't see that it makes any difference at all. Mangoes, pineapples—what're you getting so het up about?"

I don't know. For some reason it disturbs me, profoundly, when a story gets changed. I can see Wade now, in my mind's eye, first trying to peel the pineapple, and then giving up and slicing the fruit through, and through, saying, "We'll just eat 'em like orange quarters, right mate?"

Mangoes, indeed. (It's like Wilma Vance, who takes stories and alters them to fit her poems: like the day we lost Colin, when he was two, alerted all the neighbours and called the police, and then found him asleep under his bed. Wilma's poem has it that she found him, sleeping under her kitchen table, and she even remembers what he said as she brought him home.)

As the day of my trip to Africa drew closer, I suddenly remembered another old friend, Wesley Moore, and the Vancouver Public Library yielded his address in Lancashire, just outside Blackpool. For four years he taught with me at the school at Kikuyu. We were neighbours on the school compound and in the evenings we played Casino, and Monopoly and other vacuous games, while our wives talked. And one night, we played hookey: "Let's abandon the women, and go to the flicks!" I suggested, and we did. We were so late that I thought I'd better take the short cut to town, even though it was a dirt road. Seat belts had just come in then, and I had spent my weekends installing them in all my friends' cars. I remember strapping myself in tightly in the little Morris Minor, yelling at Wesley to hurry up, and then barrelling off down the road at a dangerous clip.

We went underneath the railway bridge, and I sped up over a slight rise to the north of Gichongo village, and as the headlights began pointing downward on the other side, I made out the most horrible thing: lying in the middle of the dirt road was a mongrel bitch and several puppies. She tried to scramble up, puppies hanging from her teats, and I tried to brake, but it was useless on that dirt surface. We skidded right through, and there was one loud bang, and several other muffled sounds of impact.

I felt absolutely sick. Running over dogs is not that uncommon in rural Africa, but the fact of the puppies, the fact that she was actually feeding them in the road made it so much worse. The fact that we were whites in the middle of the Kikuyu Reserve in the dark of night gave the situation a bit of an edge.

We got out and stood beside the car looking back. In the dim moonlight, we could see the mother was dead, and so were three of the puppies. Another was dragging a broken thigh in the dust, and one lay curling back and forth in pain, squealing.

"Wesley, there's no alternative, I've have to put them out of their pain," I said. We got back in the car, and I reversed, and then came forward again, crushing the two live pups under the front wheel. Then I got out and dragged all the corpses to the side of the road. And then came the worst part of all: as we drove off, I noticed, standing high above the roadway on a bank of earth, there was a silent Kikuyu boy about twelve years old, wearing just a piece of cloth, knotted at the shoulder, his hand clutching an upright walking stick.

How that night has lived with me, over the years! With the hindsight of today, one thinks of trying to save the injured pups; getting out and talking to the boy (were they his, was the bitch his own pet?) One thinks of going back the next day, and meeting the people, and talking the matter out, even paying a few shillings reparation. I didn't do any of those things. I went to my Kikuyu colleague Peter Mwangi, and told him what had happened, and asked his advice.

"Alistair!" he said, with a big thump on my back, "It's not your fault, my friend. Anyone who allows dogs to lie in the middle of the road is asking for trouble."

"But—"

"*Si 'neno! Si 'neno, bwana!* Just forget about it!"

So here I am, all these years later, driving up from London to visit Wesley. I had had one day left in my schedule, and I phoned, and he invited me up. Crazy! Four hundred and fifty kilometres in one day, and back the following day, to catch the plane home. I had known it was

98

just the kind of madcap trip that would appeal to my friend Esther, who happened to be in London at the time. Here we are barrelling along the M6, feeling nervous about driving on the wrong side of the road, and determined to get off the Motorway soon, and drift along on more pleasant roads, out of the path of the speeding semi-trailers—juggernauts, as the British call them.

I had told Esther about the puppies, and she berated me. No, she did not accept that those times were different. Killing that boy's pet dog and her puppies—and then rolling back and forth to crush the survivors—"I'm sorry, but I just think worse of you for it. It's a ghastly story."

"I know. But that *was* the rule in those days. If you injured a dog badly, you stopped and put it out of its misery. One time, when I was nineteen, driving through Tanganyika, I hit a great big pie dog, and broke both its back legs, and I had to get out and take a tire iron to it, and smash its skull. It's what we were taught. It's what we had to do, Esther."

"It's just disgusting. No wonder the Africans rebelled, and got their independence. They must have hated you. And I would've too."

"Well, it had nothing to do with hatred. Jesus, *we* weren't hated. Are you kidding? Teachers? *Waalimu?* We were held in the highest possible regard. Especially somebody like Wesley. I mean he's a real dedicated servant of the people. After Kikuyu, he took a posting to a poor, remote little school at the coast, where he saw the need was greatest."

"Hmm," said Esther, and stared out the window. She was silent for a good hour after that.

Wesley was unchanged: the same old roly-poly, fuzzy, teddybear of a man. His smile beamed delight, still a Christian, not doctrinaire, but broad, humane, a loving man. He was now a principal of a huge Secondary Modern.

"And what about the punkers?" I asked. "Do you allow all that."

He laughed. "I draw the line at boys wearing jewelry in

their ears," he said. "I've got a whole drawerful of earrings."

"And the parents and the School Board let you get away with that, in these times?"

"Oh yes! Gotta have some sort of discipline. Gotta draw the line somewhere."

We went for Chinese food, and after we ordered, we began reminiscing. Remember Monopoly? Remember Casino? Remember old Jed Quimby? Then Wesley said:

"There's one thing I'll never forget. I've often wondered if you remember it as vividly as I do, Alistair. Do you remember that night we went to town—"

"To the movies."

"Yup. To the movies."

"I know what you're going to say. Dear God, do I remember it!"

"And we came over that rise on the Dagoretti road, and we ran over those ducklings."

"Ducklings?"

"Yeah."

"And the mother duck too?" I asked.

Wesley cocked his head, and narrowed his eyes, trying to recall. "I don't remember a mother duck. I *do* remember the ducklings. It was so awful!"

"Wesley," I said. "Kikuyu people don't keep ducks—at least I never saw any that did. There's no water for them round there at Gichongo village, and Dagoretti. Anyway, ducks don't go wandering around the countryside at night. They hide, they huddle up and take shelter. Those weren't ducklings, man, they were puppies. Remember? And the mother dog."

A look of horror transformed Wesley's face.

"Anyway," said Janet, Wesley's wife, "we want to hear all about Canada now, so come on!"

Driving back to London next day, I didn't feel able to bring the matter up again, but Esther did, herself.

"He's such a nice man!" she said. "You can tell from the way he's changed that story. Somehow, it's just less brutal.

Dogs are our friends, but we eat ducks and chickens. He can't accept what really happened. Quietly, over the years, while he was asleep probably, he's dreamed-in the substitution."

It was true. I drove for a while in silence.

"'Such a nice man,' I teased her. You just want him to divorce his wife and marry you."

She smiled her crazy smile. "That might make an interesting change too," she said.

MOTORTHERAPY

I met Maxwell Eastman in 1972, in the library of
Tonawanda Community College, Lockport, N.Y. I remember
this big guy in a denim shirt getting up to shake my hand,
and holding it as he looked into my face with soft, marbled
blue eyes. His teeth showed beneath his smile, his face a
bit fat, mustache curling below his lips. His suede jacket
seemed to smell faintly of marijuana. Within the first sentence or two, he laughed.

My wife and I had driven across the continent from
Vancouver B.C., for a year's teaching exchange. I was thirty-
four, with long hair and a black beret; Christina was nineteen, in faded jeans, yellow gorilla stompers and a skimpy
halter top that drew men's eyes. We'd been warned there
were no apartments in Lockport, but we hadn't believed it.
So we were stuck in the Crittenden Motel on Route 93, until
Max offered us a room in his apartment, and we became
friends.

Ask in Lockport today, and they will tell you we developed a special friendship, not entirely understood.
Attraction of opposites? Not that simple. I think of my hat:

before we left Lockport to come home, the four of us went for a walk one day, and Christina suddenly reached up and took my old Kenya Regiment hat off my head and put it on Max's.

"What? Is this for me?" he said.

"Yes," said Christina.

"Really?"

"Of course!" I said, as though we had prearranged it. Actually, that hat was the one Kenyan thing I'd held onto, and Christina's giving it away on impulse shocked me. It took a while, but now I'm glad she did. Other events have superseded the giving of the hat, and anyway it suited him. Three years ago, when Max lay in delirium on his sickbed in Buffalo, I got the message to phone him. His daughter answered guardedly, "May I ask who's calling?" I said my name and she cried, "Oh thank God!" with a burst of emotion that quite astonished me.

That afternoon in 1972, Christina and I moved in to Max Eastman's two-bedroom apartment on the upper floor of a house beside a gas station. We lugged our stuff up, and I said, "Max, what are all these dead flies doing in the stairwell?"

"Aren't they something?" He laughed his deep, prolonged chortle, and that's when I knew we would be friends.

Max cooked, and I drove out and bought some good wine. When dinner was ready, Max lit candles and put on the record player. "You know Tom Rush?" he asked, and we shook our heads. "Listen to this."

We paid attention to the words of "No Regrets." Outside, traffic was an occasional swish of air. Inside, the candle flames glowed ruby in our wineglasses. As the song ended, I saw that Max was crying.

"What's the matter, Max?" Christina asked.

"Gaad!" He sniffed deeply. "I'm sorry."

We talked about relationships gone wrong: his divorce, his three children living in Buffalo with their mother; my divorce, my three children. "Just about everybody I know's divorced," Max said.

"Not I!" said Christina.

"Yeah," said Max. "Here's to love!" He clinked his wine-glass with ours, and Tom Rush began singing Joni Mitchell's "The Circle Game." We talked till we were all exhausted. A channel of intimacy opened that night, and never closed.

We stayed a month with Max, then moved to a house in Millersport. Sunday mornings, Max and his girlfriend Valerie would come for cream scones and strawberry jam. We went to restaurants in Buffalo, art galleries, concerts, movies. The next May, our house owners returned from Florida, and by then Max had moved into half of an old brick farmhouse on Putnam Road, and he invited us to spend the last month there. Sometimes the four of us would walk out back around the woodlot and the pond, throwing sticks into the grass for the dog. Other times, Max and I would go and help John Yeoman, the farmer, with barn chores. The old man was not keen to have us around his cows, but one day he let me carry a bucket of milk across the slippery floor to the churn, and Max congratulated me with a wink.

We invited Max and Valerie to visit us in Vancouver, the following summer. In the CN station, suddenly, there was my Kenya Regiment hat coming down the platform. We rented a cabin up at Lac Lejeune and went fishing. At a gas station I picked up a red plastic gallon can, and exclaimed at the price. Max took the can out of my hand and paid for it. When they went home, I was surprised at my feelings. We had been in agreement on all the issues, from Watergate and the bombing of Cambodia to Trudeau's Just Society. But on the little stuff we fought. Should we take the short cut or the scenic route to Lac Lejeune? Go out to eat or stay home? Which movie? More than once I said privately to Christina, "Christ I'll be relieved when Max goes home!" But at the airport, watching his big, broad shoulders move away, still smelling his hug, I felt a pang.

Some letters passed between us. Little things would

remind me of him. Once, Tom Rush came to town on my birthday, and Christina took me to hear him. "Play 'No Regrets'!" I called several times from our table in the dinner-theatre, and Tom Rush scowled at me, but at the end he announced, "This is for a friend," and plucked his guitar, and sang in his deep, voice:

I know your leaving's too long overdue
For far too long I've had nothing new
    to show to you . . .

Afterwards, I found a phone booth. It was midnight here, three in the morning in Lockport, and I could hear thunder raging.

"You always seem to call when there's a storm," Max said.

"Did I wake you up? I should have waited till morning."

"Do what's in your heart!" he said. "I'm truly glad you called."

He did not tell me then that he had broken up with Valerie. I didn't tell him that Christina and I were having difficulties. Once, I went to Toronto for a conference, and took an extra day and visited Max in Lockport. We ate a meal, and filled one another in on the latest news. A year later Max phoned, and said he wanted to come out again to Vancouver, with Sonia, Valerie's best friend, who worked in the library with him. Oh brave new Me Generation, what a carousel!

We caught the ferry to Victoria, and the Butchart Gardens. We took my boat up Indian Arm. We dived into the clear water, and I remember his great shout of protest at the cold when we broke surface. Back in the house, we lived, as always, in the kitchen, drinking wine and telling stories. Then they were gone.

Year after year, why did we make those long hauls across the continent, to plonk ourselves down across the table, only to start bitching? Could one not talk into the night and take day trips with somebody who lived closer? Oh Maxwell, you and your stubborn refusal to overlook any unresolved emotional issue! All your touchy-feely crap, right down to those haiku you went and wrote to reconcile yourself to dying:

A pear, mostly green
Sitting in the winter sun.
Through a door, the snow.

The flute speaks no words
But says that happy and sad
Are close together.

All due respect, my friend, but horseshit! How about some "rage against the dying of the light"? There is no opposing presence here to say my thoughts are wrong.

When Max and Sonia got married, they took sailing lessons, and used her parents' cash gift to buy a 25-ft sailboat they called "The Runcible Spoon." When I visited, we drove up to Lake Ontario to see it. Max seemed confident about sailing. "Sh!" he'd say, turning up the car radio. "Let's get the weather. Maybe we can sail up to Toronto."

Propped up on land for winter storage, "The Runcible Spoon" seemed a pretty substantial vessel, but I was glad when Sonia wrote later to say they'd sold it and bought a grand piano. I arrived one day on a surprise visit, hitch-hiked out to Yeomans' and was walking up the driveway, when I heard piano notes coming from the house. It was early spring, and the stench of manure in the cold air cut my nostrils, taking me back to childhood on African farms.

I opened the rickety side door, without knocking.

The Bach minuet abruptly stopped, and Max called out, "Who's this?"

"Hi Max."

He entered the kitchen, and stood for several seconds with his eyes widening and closing. He looked pale.

"What's going on?" I asked, at the kitchen table, but he resisted an answer. Then, he latched onto a thread and began telling me, frowning, how he had gone to start his car, and it wouldn't turn over. He called the Head Librarian and said, "Maureen, my car's dead, I'm not sure when I'll be in." A few minutes later Maureen called back to say she'd spoken to the Dean, and Max was to take sick leave and get some help.

"So . . . . How long does this disability leave last? Have you gotten help?"

"Gaad, Alistair, I've been sitting here for four days, helping John with the chores, practising piano and guitar."

"Let's go to New Hampshire," I said. "See Jed."

"I would *love* to see Jedediah," Max said. "But the College?"

"Not to worry," I said. "I'll call Nathan and tell him I'm taking care of it. He can tell the Dean."

I phoned my old ally in the English Department at TCC. I called Vancouver, and arranged for a colleague to cover my classes. We left a note for Sonia saying when we'd be back. As we climbed into his Saab, Max asked, "What did you tell Nathan?"

"I told him the doctor has prescribed motortherapy for you, and I am giving you a hand."

For the first time that day, Max laughed.

"How about the old road to Utica?" I said. "Then up through the Adirondacks."

"That'll take forever," he said.

"'It's got to be the going, not the getting there, that's good.'"

"Harry Chapin," Max said, and laughed again. "Motortherapy! 'The doctor has prescribed motortherapy'!"

"Hey! My Ph.D. finally pays off!"

At first we spoke little. The sun was bright, the car ran well, and I felt the excitement of skipping out. But soon we were locked in argument. He told me that since his marriage to Sonia, his daughters wouldn't visit him. His son, yes, but not his daughters. He took them out for hamburgers.

"That's weird," I said. "Is it a Catholic thing?"

"What do you mean 'weird'? Why do you say 'Catholic'? Gaad, Alistair, you're one abrasive son of a bitch!"

"Look," I said, "children have their own lives. They notice what their parents *do* for them. They're not interested in reasons."

"What are you saying?"

I felt good because he was fighting. Earlier, in his kitchen, his face had opened and closed helplessly. Now, his grip on the wheel was firm, twisting back and forth. What is our life anyway but a continuous conversation, sometimes easy and sometimes not? We were arguing whether or not to go via the Ticonderoga ferry, when he suddenly cried "Shit!" whether at something in the road, or a missed appointment, or a spasm in his back muscles, I don't know. But I felt his energy then.

At Jed's house in Concord, we drank wine and talked late. Emily, Jed's wife, excused herself and went to bed. I asked Jed about his arrangements to have his daughter by his first wife come from England for a visit. Jed was evasive.

"Your daughter's *got* to know your feelings about this, Jed," I said. "No point pussyfooting around it: the mother thinks the ex-husband is nothing but an asshole, and so will the child. You've got to act to counter that impression."

Jed frowned.

"Alistair you're a fascist!" Max cried. Jed's gotta do this, I gotta do that, my daughters have gotta come to my house."

"What's this?" Jed asked, and Max explained.

"*I* can understand that!" Jed said, his deep moral voice sounding incongruously like Richard Nixon's. "*I* can understand that Max's daughters might feel protective of their mother and not wish to come to the house of his new wife."

"What if they say no," Max asked. "Do I kidnap them?"

"People don't live forever," I said. "How long can you afford to postpone these relationships? Your eldest girl is what, sixteen?"

"Sixteen!" cried Jed. Clearly he had been thinking she was six or eight.

A look of disappointment came over Max's face. His unexpected ally had deserted. "Let's talk about something else," he said.

"Wait!" Jed insisted. "Let's see what the expert says."

I thought he was going to wake Emily, but he came back holding a letter. It was from me. He read out a paragraph in which I told Jed how one day my eldest son had preferred to work with his stepfather rather than come camping with me, and I had stood with my son on the lawn and said, "Do whatever you decide to do, without apology to anyone."

I took the letter from Jed to read.

"Now Al-istairr," Jed said, imitating the Old Man we taught under in Africa, "Al-istairr, I want you to apologise to Max. Tell him his children can do whatever they want. Without apologizing to anyone. Including you!"

"Son of a bitch!" I said.

Around 3 a.m., when I lay down to sleep on the foamy under Jed's chipped grand piano in the study, I looked across, and saw Max Eastman lying totally relaxed on his back, with the Kenya Regiment hat on his head.

When Max next arrived in Vancouver, alone, my son Colin and I got into a shouting match at supper. Max scraped back his chair: "I wanna know just *where in the hell you think you get off*, telling me how to deal with my children, when you yell at your own son like that!"

"Colin can keep his end up," I said.

"That doesn't make it any less sick!"

After Max went home, my son told me that as they walked to the store together for ice-cream, Max said to him:

"Listen, *Callin*, here's my number in New York, and if you ever need to call, call collect."

Another year, driving from Boston to Toronto, I called Sonia at TCC from the Thruway. I knew they had split up. She told me how to get to the property Max had bought in

Millersport. "Good for you, Max!" I cried, as I entered the greenhouse he was renovating to live in.

He took me out back to walk through several acres, wooded and leafy, with a pond. It was alive with birds and small animals. Then he put me to work stapling pink insulation to the walls.

"What made you suddenly decide to buy a piece of property?" I asked.

Max sat down and sighed. His big face started going through a succession of frowns and relaxations, and I thought I was going to get some Buddhist stuff. Instead he said:

"Nodal lymphoma."

"Cancer?"

"Yes."

"Well. . . . Are you going to let it kill you?"

He laughed. "No," he said. "I'm not thinking about dying."

After supper, and my latest stories from Vancouver, Max said, "You remember when you came, and I was depressed, and we visited Jed?"

"Motortherapy?"

"Yeah. You remember how I sometimes put on events in the library? Well, I put on this show of paintings by a local artist. We hung it, there was an opening, lunch-hour talk, visits from classes, so on. Afterwards, I realized *nobody* said *anything* to me about that show, good or bad. It was as though it had never happened. Apparently, it made not a jot of difference to anybody's life. Not one single person. That was a very strange feeling."

"That's when—"

"Next day, the car wouldn't start."

In the summer of 1986, Max came to Vancouver for Expo. He stayed in our rec room, and spent time in meditation. He reestablished his bond with my son Colin, whose new name, Chuck, he accepted without a qualm. I was preoccupied, writing a book. By the time I took him to the airport, several visits had blurred into one, and I thought of him as a fixture.

Two years later, Laura and I rented a cottage on Skaha Lake, for a water-skiing holiday. On impulse, I called Max in Millersport, and invited him to join us.

"Water-ski? Gaad, Alistair, there's nothing I'd like better. Maybe I can come."

"Come!"

"Well. I might not be able to."

"What's the matter?"

"Well, shit, the thing has come back."

"*Drive* it away, Max. Water-skiing is so beautiful. Think about ballet man, just gliding over the water."

"I'll let you know," he said.

Jed called me a few days later to say Max was sick. Then Max called and said he definitely could not come water-skiing.

"Look," I said, "you told me once that you were not going to let this thing kill you. So just come!"

I handed the phone to Laura, and heard her say, "It doesn't help when people are denying."

When she hung up, she said, "Nobody's denying it around there. His daughter has quit her job to be with him. The whole family's, there. He's at his first wife's place."

"Therese's?"

"Yes."

"Where's Sonia?"

"She's there all the time."

I tried to absorb this information while I slept.

In the morning, I said: "Max Eastman is such a one for feelings, you know, theatre of the self. He'll spend a year at this, people round his bedside, Anthea quitting her job, dramatic phone calls."

"Call and tell him!"

"No. If he decides to live, he'll fly out here."

Next night, when I got home, Laura said Jed had called,

and would call again at nine. I ate supper and waited. Jed sounded shook-up. He was on the road home from visiting Max in Lockport, and finding it difficult to drive.

I said sternly, "You've done what you can. Life's for the living, man. Concentrate on getting home. Tomorrow you can write your feelings down."

Early next morning, Max Eastman died. At the end of the week, Sonia phoned us, and later sent a copy of the memorial service, including Max's four haiku. Jed wrote his letter. He thought it was too raw, but after a month he sent it. He described Max lying in an overheated room, naked on a sheepskin, recognizing people who leaned in to tell the dying man they loved him. He cried for music, and they put on Vivaldi. "No," he demanded, "rock and roll!" so they put on a Dylan record. But it had barely begun, when he shouted "Stop it! Take it off!" Although he was terminally weak, he was anxious to hear what people had to say to him. He listened attentively to their voices in the room, and on the phone.

"The pavement seemed straighter, flatter, blacker on the drive home," Jed wrote. "All the dimensions of life seemed to withdraw from their loveliness. Hot sun, black pavement, people running around . . . all seemed remotely bizarre; the cars, the people. the traffic lights, the bricks and mortar and tin and sticks that people have erected . . . . All terribly silly, vain, and of no real importance."

Early next spring, I made it to Lockport once again. Sonia put on her camel-hair coat and took me out to Max's former property in Millersport. As she drove, she confessed, "You know, Alistair, when we had the boat, and Maxwell would be listening to the weather to see if we could go out across the lake, I always prayed it would be stormy!" She laughed, and sniffed back a tear. I took her hand and held it for a moment, and then we drove on.

At Millersport, we asked permission of the young man who lives there now to walk in back to the pond.

"This is where we scattered his ashes," Sonia said.

There was a derelict wooden chair in the snow, over-grown with grass, facing the water. We stood beside it in silence and I looked down into the clear, glassy pond, and just for a moment felt Max's presence there between us.

I blinked, and looked again, and saw no more than the bright surface of water and reflections of bare trees.

VERSABRAILLE

More than once, at bedtime, my father lay on the mat between our beds, and told my brother and me a story about our blind uncle James:

"At the School for the Blind, at Worcester in the Cape," he said, "James and four of his mates decided to play truant and go swimming in the river."

"How old was he, Dad?"

"Oh, he would have been about nine or ten . . . ."

We came to know the story well. The blind boys take their clothes off, and jump in where they are sure the water is deep. Their clothes are stolen. Oblivious, they swim, and when they have had their fill of it, they climb out, and grope around on the bank. No clothes. They feel shame. They cover themselves with their hands. They decide to hide under the bridge till nightfall. Five naked blind boys creep stealthily through the dark town, and break in to their dormitory. They are caught, and caned. They are threatened with expulsion. Sternly, they are told they must work off the value of the lost clothing, which they do over the next year.

And then, to round the story off, and leave us feeling tranquil for the night, my father would tell of the advantage James had by being blind: "At lights-out he could just go on reading! We'd all have to put our books away, and there James would be with his Braille book under the blankets, chuckling away to himself."

As a child, that was all I knew about Uncle Jim. Now he is 85, and still active. He has lived most of his life in Cape Town, where, before he retired, he had a thriving physio therapy practice. Early each morning, he'd walk down Rondebosch Road to the station, and take the suburban train to town. Then up the length of Adderly Street to his office. From there he also travelled to patients in three separate hospitals, one of which was at least a mile from the train. I don't know how, but he managed all this without complaint or apparent difficulty, and in his spare time he crusaded for the blind, and was specially interested in ways to make them independent.

Even though he was my godfather, and his name is my middle one, I was born in Kenya, so I didn't even meet Uncle Jim till I went down to the Cape to University. Then, I was more interested in girls than a blind uncle, and visited him only a couple of times. He smoked cigarettes, and I would watch with concern as he waved his fourth finger incessantly to and fro across the red tip, to knock off any ash. After getting my B.A., I left Cape Town and went back home to Kenya, and later I emigrated to Canada, so Uncle Jim faded in memory. Once, as a graduate student at UBC, when I was undergoing the notorious required course in research and bibliography, I decided to search for an article I'd heard Uncle Jim had written about blindness. But to my amazement, it was my own name I found listed in the *Index to South African Periodicals*—my first published story, and I hadn't even known about it! I forgot Uncle Jim for the time being.

He was seventy-seven when I next saw him, and he told me he was raising money to buy Versabraille machines.

"We could probably have raised quite a lot more by now," he said, with a bitter edge to his voice, "if I hadn't had to spend so much of my energy speaking out against guide dogs!"

"What's the matter with guide dogs, Uncle Jim?"

"Nothing!" he said. "They're fine animals." And then, after a storyteller's pause, he added: "Only trouble is, they don't live to be threescore and ten, you know. Twelve or thirteen years, and they kick the bucket. Meanwhile the blind person's that much older, and believe you me, it's not easy to adapt to a new dog. No, man, having a dog cramps your style in the end. I know quite a few blind people who're homebound now, because their second or third dog died. A Versabraille's a hell of a lot more worth having."

We were sitting in the crowded living-room of my half-brother's little house in Cape Town. A dozen of my relatives had assembled, for I had been in Canada over twenty years, and this was my first trip back to Africa. It was a marvellous evening, full of stories.

I told one on myself: how that afternoon, I had walked through the Gardens at the top of Adderly Street, past the old Parliament Buildings, and felt comfortably over-whelmed by the history of the place. I was able to put aside for a moment *apartheid*, and all South Africa's woes, and take a simple pleasure in thinking that it was right here, a hundred years ago, that two of my great-grand-fathers had been eminent politicians; and the oak trees on either side had been planted by Simon van der Stel a good two-and-a-half centuries before *that*. But the serenity of the old oak avenue was suddenly shattered by the bark of mili-tary orders:

"Left-right! Left-right!
Pick-up-those-shoulders! Swing-those-arms!
You in the third rank, step out of file!"

("Third *rank*"! It sounded like "third *Reich*"!) When I turned to look, the sight was more horrible than the sound because I saw that they were women. White schoolgirls in blue-green uniform tunics, marching stiffly under the oaks, as prefects barked commands at them in a harsh stream, bordering on insult. Then I saw other girls walking quietly home through the gardens in similar uniforms. School was out. I had to know: What was this Hitler-Youth affair. I approached a girl walking alone.

"Excuse me," I said, with a deliberate smile. "Can you tell me what these girls are doing?"

The young student frowned, and looked where I pointed. She narrowed her eyes and frowned again.

"Is it a punishment?" I suggested softly.

She concentrated yet again, puzzled, then her frown broke.

"Auw no," she said. "These girls, they wanna be drum-majorettes."

As I told the punchline of the story, my relatives all laughed. Fancy the ignorant Canadian liberal mistaking the cheerleaders for Nazis! "Good thing you're able to laugh at yourself!" said my cousin Chloe, Uncle Jim's daughter.

"That reminds me," said Uncle Jim, taking the floor, and he told about a patient who came to see him once in his office.

"Why do you want to see me, particularly?" Uncle Jim asks.

"I'm convinced you're the only physio in town who can help me."

"Fine," says Uncle Jim. "Go in and undress. Put on the gown that's hanging behind the door, and lie on the table."

"Yes, but there's something I have to tell you. I'm not White, you see. I'm Coloured."

"Well," says Uncle Jim, "that doesn't matter to me, because *I* can't tell the difference!"

Everyone laughed briefly. Watching his little body sitting erect in the soft chair, I could tell Uncle Jim was disappointed. He reached into his mind for a better story. It occurred to me suddenly that *he* is the family story-teller. Of course! If I was blind, wouldn't I live even more in the language in my head? The words and images constantly swirling around in Uncle Jim's imagination must provide him with a necessary universe.

Uncle Jim cannot remember actually seeing things. But he was not born blind. When he was two, they dilated his pupils to check the eyes, and a nurse misread the doctor's instructions, and took the bandages off too soon. The sensitized retinas burned.

His parents accepted his blindness, and gave no thought to suing. They arranged for him to have piano lessons. Did they hope that he might be able to earn a living as a concert pianist, or were they just trying to give him a gift, something extraordinary that he could become good at, and feel a measure of control over? I don't know. After he passed the Conservatory grades, they sent him for physiotherapy training. Was that their plan or his? Either way, it worked. Meanwhile, his father, a magistrate, never got a big city posting, but stayed content at little towns in the Cape.

"Your father doesn't seem to have been ambitious, Uncle Jim," I say, "is that right? I mean your *grandfather*, the Colonel was famous for his speeches in Parliament, and everything else. They closed the city of Cape Town for his funeral, and the Prime Minister acted as a pallbearer. But your father never seems to have made it past Tulbagh and Stutterheim. I don't hear much about him."

I've been distracted by my own question, but, now that I look at Uncle Jim, I see a wave passing over his face like a pale flash of anger. He has drawn himself even more erect in his chair.

"My father," he declares, in that stern, proud Randall voice which connects itself to all the decencies of life, and then clears its throat as a brook against criticism, "my father gave us all a name to live *up to!*" He ends this with what sounds to me like an accusatory emphasis. Is he thinking of my having departed to Canada? My divorce? Perhaps I imagine these things. Certainly, I came to the critical realization quite young that for my father's family, the world

119

was divided into two types of people: Randalls, and others.

And then Uncle Jim smiles, and begins:

One day, when he was seven years old, and the family was living in Tulbagh, his father called him into his study.

"James, I want you to go to town and get something for me, all right?"

"*Me*, Dad?" the blind boy protests. "But I've never *been* that far on my own before!"

"Come, come, you're old enough," his father says adamantly. "Off you go and buy me two ounces of Rum and Maple at the tobacconist."

"*Ag* Daddy, how will I know the shop?"

"You'll smell it, man! Here's the money. Go now. I'll be in my study when you come back."

The terrified little boy, with a shilling tight in his left hand, tap-taps his cane along fences, then tall grass and ditches, block after block. He stands at the side of the road wondering if he dare cross. The clopping of horses' hooves is mixed in with the rumble of wagon wheels, and a chudder of Model Ts. Little James can't separate out the sounds enough to get the picture. Finally, he takes a deep breath, holds his white stick high in the air, and marches slowly, determinedly across the road. Terrified! He hears a car motor coming louder, nearer. He raises the cane as high as he possibly can. His ears are pounding; he cannot tell if that car has stopped, or what. Finally, he feels the roadbed sloping down. Excited, he stumbles into the curb, and falls forward, almost flat on his face, but luckily, manages to catch his balance. He stops and turns his face around, around. His father was right. He can smell tobacco, and he moves towards the smell until he's there. He buys the Rum and Maple and begins the return, with pounding heart. Eventually, his hand touches the carved, wooden gatepost of home. The blind boy enters his father's study holding up a small jute bag in triumph. "I brought your tobacco, Dad!"

"Thanks. Just put it on the table by the door, please. And you can keep the change as your reward." The old man does not get out of his chair.

That was 1914. Twenty-one years later, his father lay dying, and James sat beside him at his sick-bed, holding his hand. "Dad," he said, "you know that time you sent me to buy tobacco when I was just a little boy? That was the *best* thing you ever did for me, huh. It taught me self-reliance, and at just the right age too. I owe you a ton for that. All that I've managed to do in my life. But, oh *boy*, was I scared. And, you know Dad, I realized recently: I *was* only seven then. Do you not think you were taking a bit of a risk?"

The old man waited a moment, then put his hand up on his son's shoulder. "My boy," he said, "I didn't tell you this before. But I can tell you now. When you went for that tobacco, I was two paces behind you, every step of the way."

After the family get-together in 1984, I said goodbye to Uncle Jim, thinking it would be the last time I'd ever see him. I was wrong. I went back to Cape Town two years later to research a historical novel, and in due course found myself a sort of guest of honour at a dinner at cousin Chloe's, amid a throng of relatives. Ursula, Chloe's mother, warned me not to refer to the mushrooms being served. "Grampa doesn't like mushrooms," she explained, and I wondered what sinister tale of poisoning might lie behind that fact.

After dinner of salmon and lamb (and the unmentionable mushrooms), Uncle Jim ensconced himself in an easy chair, with a small glass of red wine and began to hold forth. Age was making him bolder. He railed over a man who had traded on his blindness for sympathy ("I'd go to jail for slander if I spilled out everything I think about *that* bastard!") He told the famous story about skinny-dipping with his blind schoolmates at Worcester when someone stole their clothes. And then, remembering all of a sudden how I had called his father's memory into question two years before, he turned to me sharply and said, "Those little towns in the Cape that you mentioned, Tulbagh, and Stutterheim, and so forth, where Dad was magistrate: you look on a map, and see where Worcester is."

I didn't need the map. I understood immediately. Those small towns form a ring around Worcester. My grandfather had not sought promotion—probably had turned it down more than once—so that the family could stay close to the Blind School. ("You know, magistrates were not paid very well in those days," my father used to say, to explain why he relied on a maternal uncle, rather than his parents, to send him through law school. But now I understood what my father possibly didn't: maybe magistrates were paid *quite well* enough, but this one had expensive priorities.) There were six other children (and another had died) but James's needs took first place. I thought better of my grandfather when I understood that. I wished that he had lived long enough for me to meet him.

In August, 1987, Uncle Jim turned eighty. Oldest member of the family. My cousins decided it was an important occasion, and should be marked. When I got home, my wife said that B.C. Tel had called to book a conference call two weeks ahead.

"Damn it! I'll be on Galiano that day!"

"I gave them that number."

"But the Gulf Islands' phone lines are down half the time!"

It was complicated, but in the end some two dozen of us were hooked up across the world on one line. The phone call became totally frustrating: all you could do was listen. My cousin Catherine in Bulawayo was emceeing the show. She said, "Are you there, Calvin, in Surrey?" And he said, "Yes, hullo, I'm here." "Barbara in Cornwall, are you there?" "Yes, I'm here. Hullo Jim." "Are you there Mike and Sally in Durban?" "Yes, we're here." "Aunt Elizabeth in East London, are you there?" "I'm here, yes, hullo James." "Alistair, are you there in Canada?" "I'm here, yes, hullo Uncle Jim."

"*Hull-o-o!*" he growled as he recognized one name or another. "Dennis, in Cape Town, are you there?" "Ya!"

Hullo and *I'm here* were the sum total of our communication with one another, in ten minutes of expensive international hookup. We tried to sing Happy Birthday, but the fractional time delays caused by the satellites in the system turned it into a hullabaloo. Having established the link, it was all over. Happy Birthday. I'm here! *Line goes dead.*

And yet it was magic. All these bits of our family scattered around the world being connected to one another, for a few minutes over a telephone. (We never did manage to get the Australian relatives on the line.) When it was over, I put down the phone and burst into tears.

A few days later, I decided to call Uncle Jim myself. That way at least I could say something personal. I switched my phone from "tone" to "pulse," because somebody told me there's less chance of a wrong number that way. Carefully, I pressed the numbers of the country code, the city routing, the number. Nothing. Then there started a very noisy, urgent double ring, but no-one answered. Then a taped message came on, and I couldn't catch the Afrikaans. The English told me the line had been disconnected.

Disconnected! What a sinister euphemism! I felt a shame come over me, as though I had killed Uncle Jim. Then I pulled myself together and called his daughter's number.

Uncle Jim was tired, Chloe said. They'd decided to move him out of his apartment, into a room in their house. Yes, I could speak to him, but right now he was lying down. Could I call in an hour?

But an hour later the line was bad, or his hearing was weak. He kept shouting "What's that? Come again?" He didn't seem very interested.

I summoned my powers of enunciation, and said as distinctly as I have ever spoken: "Do you mind, Uncle Jim, if I write that story about your father sending you to get tobacco?"

"Write any story you darn well please!" he shouted back. Then, after a pause, he said, in a sharp, clear voice, "Look here, man, if you get any money out of it, make sure you send me a donation for the Lighthouse Club. We've got six Versabrailles on order, and no cash to pay for them."

"Yeah, yeah. I'll see what I can do."

"Righto," he said. And just when I meant to ask him what a Versabraille was, he hung up.

ACCIDENTS

"Do you think we'd be friends today, if it hadn't been for Wilma?"

Neil's eyes widened in that matter-of-fact way of his. "We wouldn't have met. That's all."

I thought about this. Dumb question. But Neil wouldn't have said so. He doesn't call people names. He smiled, and said he was off to Japan for a month, and when he got back he was going to try to get to Berlin.

"Damn it," I said. "I'll really miss you! And who am I going to play racquetball with?"

There are a few friendships that I consider absolute—no qualifications. Wilma tried once to resign. When her marriage broke up, she wrote me a sad letter, and at the end of my long reply I mentioned how incredible the Canada Geese were in southern Ontario where I was staying—like no other display of wild life I had ever seen, even in Africa. Wilma was so pissed off, she sent me a curt note dismissing me forever. "Anyone with so little feeling, that when I tell them my *marriage* is over, they can write back and talk about migrating birds is NO FRIEND OF MINE!" I had to laugh. In those days people still sent telegrams. Mine said "RESIGNATION DECLINED."

Two years later, back in Vancouver, I started a small press, and one day Wilma showed up with this young guy in tow. Sheepish he looked, docile behind his thick glasses.

"Alistair, this is Neil," she said. "I want you to read his poems. Give them to him." Neil dutifully passed over a folder.

"How about a glass of wine?" I said. "I can't judge properly unless I'm quite alone. I'll let you know as soon as I've read them."

Later that night after Wilma and Neil had left, I did read his manuscript. It contained some astonishingly violent images: raccoons clubbed to death, and the dismal look of their eyes; a car crash, with one of the injured thrashing about in a ditch, all bloody; a helicopter accident, where the transmission breaks up and shoots bits of mangled steel into the cabin and through the pilot's body. I was surprised at such brutal scenes coming from that reticent young man. But the writing was good, and I phoned him the next day, and told him I would publish three of his poems in a Western Canada anthology I was putting together.

Then we became friends. We play racquetball, and occasionally dine out, and several times we have gone off together, to a cabin by a lake, or to Wilma's place when she was away, to write. We've co-authored a screenplay about Canadian politics, and though no-one yet has taken it up to make into a movie, we are working on the sequel.

Of course, people look at us strangely sometimes. I was going to say that, at his wedding—make a joke—but then I decided not to. Mathilde had sent a message via Neil: "She says please don't embarrass us." The day before he had asked me, "Alistair, will you give us a toast?" and I agreed to. Next day, that worried message from Mathilde. I suppose she meant don't mention her belly. The suspicion of Neil and I being gay lovers was what I'd thought of.

"How can I roast you without embarrassment?" I asked.

126

"Toast!" he said loudly. "A *toast*."

"Thought you *said* 'roast.' Now you change it. The hell with that!"

He smiled, but looked nervous. Something about people getting married brings out this desire in us to torment them.

Not that Neil is a stranger to married life. He lived with his previous girlfriend for almost ten years, and though they never went through a ceremony, they were the most married couple I knew, never out of one another's ken—seldom even out of sight. When he won a grant to go to Berlin for a year to write a book of poems, Bronwyn quit her job and went with him.

"That seems wrong to me," I told Wilma. "Can't she leave him alone? How can he investigate the soul of an old city, with his wife tagging along?"

"She's *not* his wife!" Wilma said. "Are they married?"

"I would say so. How well do you know him?"

"I just met him accidentally. He was in a workshop I gave a talk to, and afterwards we all went for a drink."

When Neil and Bronwyn returned from Europe, something was wrong. His face had a shut look. Guilty. As though somebody had tapped him on the shoulder in an old-fashioned way: *See here, boy, don't you ever hurt that girl!* And now he knew it was happening.

"Hey, look!" I said to him one day. "Why don't I take you and Bronwyn cross-country skiing, Saturday?"

Mumble, mumble. He wasn't sure if she would want it . . . they'd never skied . . . they didn't have equipment.

"Come *on!*" I said. "Fresh air and snow. Laura and I'll pick you up. You skate, so you certainly can cross-country ski."

We went. But I had forgotten to warn them about the walk up through snow to the rental place. After parking, I looked behind and saw Bronwyn's bare feet in wooden clogs. I locked the car, and the miserable attempt began, Laura and me leading the way, Neil and Bronwyn dragging behind. At one point Laura turned to me and said, "Just leave them. Let's go and ski!"

Bronwyn's feet were cold. The rental boots didn't fit. Etcetera. Finally, Neil said, "Is there a bus down from here?" I handed him the key, and said, "You guys take the car. We'll hitch-hike down when we're through." They left, and as we watched them slink off through the trees, Laura said, "Thank God!"

But that was not the end of it. An hour later, on the powerline, I saw Neil sloping glumly along through the snow beside the trail. I skied to a turning halt beside him. "What's up, man?"

"The key broke off in the lock."

"What!"

All he had to do was stick that little key in the trunk lock and exert light finger pressure to the left, and the trunk would pop open, and there he'd have the main bunch of keys, to drive with. "The key broke off in the lock"! *Incredible*. Yet I could accept it because Laura had had difficulty before, turning the key right, right, right, and never thinking to try left.

I took the broken key stub and left him to trudge after me. I skied down to the car, and knew the solution before I got there: Stick the stub in and turn. If the broken tongue of the key was still in there, it would be holding the tumblers open. I stuck it in, turned left, and the trunk popped. Why hadn't Neil thought of that?

Bronwyn was huddled on the back seat under every stitch of clothing she had been able to find, shivering, and miserable. I started the motor and turned the heat on. By the time Neil arrived, the windows were all clear. Watching them drive away, Bronwyn still in the back, I had a feeling that relationship was finished.

Soon, Neil began showing up around supper time at our front door, holding a bottle of wine. Some people might have resented the predictable *ding-dong* of the door chime, night after night, but with us it was the opposite. Over supper, we listened to his talk (and drank his wine). But it worried us to see him so unmotivated. After doing joe work at minimum wage for years, Neil had finally landed a job as a junior reporter for the *Vancouver Sun*, but he no sooner got it than he began complaining: said he didn't know how to write stories, didn't know where to *find* stories, didn't know how to file copy that wouldn't get blue-pencilled and set his boss yelling. I wanted to take him sometimes, and give him a good shake. Once, when I went down to the TV room and interrupted the hockey game, demanding to know which of my sons had taken a shower and left the bathroom flooded, it was Neil who put his hand over his face, and went upstairs to mop the floor.

One evening, Neil and I were at the Kitsilano School of Writing, at a Board Meeting. As it came to an end he was lying like a seal on the sofa, his head resting on his fingers and his legs sticking out in front. Someone said, "Time to put castors on Neil now, and wheel him home to bed." Everyone laughed, but I worried.

Neil and Bronwyn split up, and he moved into an unfurnished apartment. At supper, I said I'd lend him stuff, and one of my sons offered: "Wanna borrow my bed? I don't mind sleeping on a foamy."

"It's all right," Neil said, "I've got a bed, and sofa and kitchen table in storage at my parents' place in Abbotsford. I'm renting a truck this weekend, to go pick them up."

"Too expensive," I said. "My car's got a hitch, we'll just rent a trailer."

"You sure?"

So on a cold Saturday in January, we drove out together on the Transcanada in my old Fiat with a huge trailer behind. It was too big for my car, according to the rental guy, who made me sign a waiver form. Driving across the Port Mann bridge, with one eye on the rear view mirror alert for signs of fishtailing, I felt incredibly happy. Neil had just turned thirty-three then, and I was twelve years older, but I felt like we were a couple of teenagers out on a lark.

Then it began to snow. The freeway took us deeper into

the storm. It came down so heavily, the wipers could barely clear it. Semi-trailer rigs began to pass us, and for long,
appalling moments the windshield would be flooded with
dark slush. When it cleared and I saw the edges again, my
heart was pounding.

"Maybe we should stop," Neil said.

"Maybe not."

Then the wipers stopped working. This had happened
before, and I knew what it was. A circlip had come off, and
the linkage had fallen apart. Not a big problem, but what
could I fashion a new clip from?

"There's a service station off the last exit," Neil said.
"Shall I walk back?"

I shook my head. "I need thin steel wire."

"Maybe in the trailer?"

I looked at him, frustrated, the way I feel sometimes
when Laura proposes a hopelessly impractical solution to a
problem.

"Sure," I said. "Take a look." I stared into the motor to
see what I could use. Neil came back in a minute or two
with a short piece of picture wire.

"Perfect!" I said. "Did you know it was there?"

"I thought something might be."

I rigged up the repair, and we set off again through even
thicker snow. An hour later we reached Abbotsford. Neil
directed me, and as I made the final turn down into a road
of deep, unploughed snow, he mumbled quickly: "It's a
cul-de-sac. I guess I should have warned you."

I changed down and the car churned, skidding and sliding. I could see the small circle at the end, and speeded up
to 25 km/h.

"I'm going to rush it," I said. "If we don't make the turn,
we'll unhitch, and then push the car and the trailer out."

"Sure."

We came to a spinning stop, halfway round the circle.
"Well, here we are!" I said with a grin, and opened my
door, and stepped into deep snow. On the roof of the

nearest bungalow, a short, stocky man stood brushing away at the snowflakes as they fell. I knew at once it was Neil's father. I had never met him, but over the years we had relayed occasional phone messages.

"Hello!" I called up. "Nice to meet you finally."

His broom stopped, and he looked down at me for a few seconds without a word. Then he said:

"You're gonna have to learn to drive in snow."

I'm gonna have to what?

The unhitching and pushing went smoothly. When we had hitched up again, I drove back and forth a couple of metres, to make a starting track for when the trailer was loaded.

Neil's mother opened the door for us, and said tea was almost ready. Then his father came down off the roof, and shook my hand. I had taken the wiper mechanism off the car, and I asked if he had a hacksaw and a vice.

"Take your shoes off and follow me," he said, and led me through the house to his workshop. "Anything you need, just call." He left me there, which struck me as odd. But then I realized he didn't want to have to stand around watching me fix the wiper. If he was going to be there, he'd have to be in charge.

After tea, we carried the furniture out to the trailer, and Neil's father supervised. "Careful . . . hold it upright . . . *don't let it touch that wall!*" He reminded me of the worst side of my own father when I was a child. He sounded like *me* bitching at my teenage sons. "Jesus, shut up, man!" I wanted to say. "I'm forty-five years old!" Instead, I concentrated on getting Neil's stuff into the trailer.

Once he was settled in his apartment, Neil's supper visits began to taper off. Months went by without our seeing him. By now my press was growing, and becoming a little bit known. We had about forty literary titles out, and though none of them sold well enough to recover its cost, the granting agencies approved of what we were doing, and gave us enough money to operate. Thank God for Laura's teaching salary, or I might have had to pack it in. Neil's second book was shortlisted for the poetry prize in the annual B.C. book awards—the first time one of our authors had been so honoured. We all went to the Gala Dinner, at the Hotel Vancouver, Laura and I, Neil and his new girl-friend Mathilde, and the three employees of the press. Nobody knew beforehand which of the finalists had won, and when Neil's name was announced, our whole table stood up and clapped, and I felt a wash of joy sweep over me.

A year later, I was editing Neil's third book and I sudden-ly missed him, so I called him and suggested we get to-gether. Yes, he said, he'd like to do that, he was thinking of taking up racquetball, did I play? No, but let's do it. As I approached fifty, enough of my friends had had triple bypass operations, or even died, that I was thinking about how the doctors always play golf, and I had taken to walk-ing long distances on any pretext. Sure! A game of racquet-ball once a week would be ideal.

We bought a rule book, and watched some play at the Community Centre, and then booked a court. The first time we played I beat him 21-7, 21-4, 21-1. The following week, he got as high as 10. It didn't matter to me who won, just sweating it out on the court made me feel great. We'd have a beer afterwards, and he'd tell me how happy his life with Mathilde was. Isn't it strange how little we know of other people's relationships? Looking in from the outside, I could not have told you the difference between his life with Bronwyn, and with Mathilde. For him, it was the difference between disaster and the marvellous. To me, it seemed quite arbitrary, a matter of accident or timing, like who wins at racquetball.

After a dozen of these weekly games, Neil suddenly improved. He drew me 20-20 one day, and I managed to squeak ahead to 22 and win. But he had had the experi-ence of being equal now, and every time we came to the court, I could sense he expected to win. Another time we got a 20-20 draw, and thrashed away for twenty minutes longer till he finally won at 28-26. Then, for eight weeks straight, he beat me every game. I didn't think anything of it, until one day, I beat him again, 21-19. Neil was furious. He knocked the wall with his $160-racquet; he kicked the door and swore. In the second game, he accidentally hit me on the shoulder blade with the ball, and it stung like hell. Quickly, he grabbed the ball and served again. One time, he hit a wall shot so hard the ball bounced back in his face and broke his glasses. On our next game, we were in the middle of a furious rally, when suddenly I found myself lying on the floor, staring up at the lights and Neil saying, "Are you okay? Are you okay?" His shot had hit me on the temple and knocked me out—something I would not have thought possible from a racquetball.

I began to feel uneasy, standing waiting for him to serve. And once, when I moved ahead from 3-3 to 6-3, I deliberately made no effort to win the next point, because I didn't want to face his anger.

For a time, I dwelled on what had happened on the racquetball court. Images of Neil would come into my mind, a different Neil than I was used to thinking of. At the lakeside cabin, when we wrote our screenplay, he used to get up every morning quite early, and go swimming. Making coffee at the kitchen sink, I'd see him way out in the middle of the still water, with rings of concentric ripples around him. He was at home in that calm, an aquatic animal enjoying his element; then, ever so slowly, he'd stretch his arms out in front and pull them aside in a steady stroke. He seemed fascinated by the water, self-sufficient and tranquil. Against that, I had the image of Neil on the racquetball court, looking alien in his new black protective eyewear; swiping at the ball, lunging to reach a drop shot—twice, three times fetching up against the court door with a slam and a loud curse. *You're going to have to learn to drive in snow!* his father growls down at me. *Take your shoes off. Follow me.*

I told Laura about Neil's violence on the racquetball court, but she just seized on it as one more reason to dismiss competitive sports. I told Wilma, and she listened, surprised. I could see she wanted to witness it for herself. I tried to bring the matter up with Neil, but he got embarrassed, and mumbled something about not meaning to be violent. So there it stayed with me, not earth-shattering, just a contradiction I couldn't quite grasp.

One day, I was reading a story by Alice Munro, and there was a line in it that struck a chord in me: about forgiveness, how children have to grow up and forgive their parents, how people have to forgive one another for being human, for carelessness, and arbitrariness, and accidents. Yes, even that stodgy curmudgeon on the roof, sweeping at snowflakes like King Canute—he needs forgiving. I suddenly realized that Neil and I had always approached one another with acceptance because there would never be anything to forgive. Even at the lake, when we argued hotly over lines in the screenplay, or in my office, when he smoked cigarettes and outraged me by stubbing them into the side of the plastic waste basket, leaving permanent black burn marks, or on other occasions where we might have come to hostilities, they never happened.

One day, after racquetball, he made a confession:

"Remember when you tried to take us cross-country skiing, and the key broke off in the lock?"

"Yeah?"

"It didn't just break off."

"No?"

"I kicked it."

I saw him instantly in my mind: all of the frustrations of the day, and finally, he inserts the key, and it won't turn: Last straw! Flash! He stands back and delivers a mighty kick, breaking the key and sending the stub spinning off into the snow. I laughed and put my arm around his shoulder.

"And it's taken you ten years to tell me?"

"Is it that long?"

A while ago Neil arrived with the news that Mathilde was four months pregnant, and they were getting married, and would I give the toast? A late first baby! Did they know what was about to hit them?

"Well, Neil," I said. "You're going to have to learn to be a father, you know."

"Yeah?" he said. "Take your *shoes* off and follow me."

THE WISHING STONE
OR
IN PURSUIT OF NATURAL KNOWLEDGE

Twenty years—twenty-two to be exact. Will I recognize him?

The crowd waiting at Heathrow's cramped Arrivals level bears densely against the trickle of passengers filtering from Customs. Several people are holding up rectangles of cardboard with names. "Mohammed Noor." "Dr. Elizabeth Wylie." "Mr. P. Fatah."

My brother was twenty-eight when I last saw him. Now he is fifty. I wonder what he looks like.

Next thing, I hear the family whistle. Calvin has seen me first; my head whips around: *there he is!* We both smile, and advance to one another across the barrier with right hands extended.

"How are *you*, Alistair? Good flight?"

"Fine, man. How are you?"

I am stunned by the power of his face, the thickening of his neck. Here I have been remembering the face of a youth, of a young man, but this tanned and mottled brow has all the authority of my father. He turns around, picking up one of my bags, and I see the leathery hatch marks on the back of his neck.

Driving away from Heathrow, my brother talks nonstop, in a loud, excited spiel filled with emphases. He switches abruptly from topic to topic as they come to him.

"Then they put the M25 through, and it was total bloody confusion. . . .

"Man, for the first time in my life, I didn't know *who* to vote for. I was *desperate* to get Maggie back in, but this local chap is absolutely *useless*. . . .

"Mama Ngina and the Family, they just *robbed* the country *blind*, man. . . ."

I can't take in all the stuff he's telling me. I notice the speed and energy of his talk, and I realize with a mild shock that he's like me—I've always been in trouble for talking too much. If this was Vancouver and I was driving, I would be doing the same thing to him. I know, because I've imagined driving him around, and my father too before he died, explaining all my landscape.

Within twenty-four hours, Calvin and I have talked more words than we ever spoke to one another in the years of growing up. We have sniffed out all each other's attitudes, and discovered that the rift that lay between us in childhood has, if anything, widened. In every way, we discover, we are opposites, different breeds of dog. More likely: if one of us is a dog, then the other's a cat. The thing that *has* changed though is that we are talking to one another. The hostile silence of childhood has gone at last. Words flow between us, like magnetic energy between opposite poles.

I have brought them maple syrup from Canada. I take over from Mary in the kitchen, and cook pancakes and bacon for my brother's family. His wife and children love them. His son and daughter pour polite trickles of syrup onto the bacon, and I take the jar and swamp their plates. Calvin declines, in favour of a poached egg, but when I have finished my plate, he gestures invitingly to his kids:

"Have some more of that stuff."

After breakfast, his son Nigel invites me in the most English of voices: "Uncle Aliss-tuh, would you like to play a com-*pu*-ter game?" I can't get over the foreignness of his voice—the pure pongo intonations that we mocked so scornfully as children growing up in Kenya.

"Sure!" I say. It is the early days of computers, and I have little experience of them.

Nigel sits absorbed in front of the screen, and I watch, trying to pick up the game. It's called "Emperor." He has to make decisions on the running of his country: how many workers to send into the fields to grow food, how many to put into the army to resist the enemy, how many to send to build dykes along the river, and so forth. I'm intrigued. What a teaching device! Here's my ten-year-old nephew wrestling with decisions of state. Each decision has a consequence, and soon it becomes evident that Nigel isn't doing too well. Furiously he punches at the keys pulling soldiers out of the army to go resist the river flooding, but oops! he hasn't reserved enough food, and his people are suffering from famine. Within three computerized months his bad decisions have cost him his kingdom. As he makes the last desperate efforts to turn the tide of disaster, a new thought occurs to me: there is something sinister in this game; so casually people can be starved, or sent to kill, or die. All just the clicking of the keyboard.

"Here," he says. "You have a go!"

My kingdom lasts a scant two weeks. Remembering how the river flooded on Nigel, I send a large force to the dykes, only to be over-run by the enemy.

Nigel chortles with superior delight: "You've lost *all* your soldiers! A thousand soldiers, dead!"

"What are their names?" I ask.

He looks at me.

"What do you mean?" he says.

He takes the keyboard now, and plays. Again, when he

loses some of his army, I push the question: "What are their names," and again he looks at me strangely, but doesn't reply.

Calvin is reading the newspaper at the dining-room table. I hear, from the way he rustles the page, that he senses I am up to something. Pretty soon we are launched into argument.

"It's *just* a game!" he protests.

"Oh yes. But don't you think it has a conditioning effect?"

He swallows. "I think you . . . look for effects that aren't there," he says, restraining himself.

By the next night, our talk is still picking up steam.

"God, it's almost three a.m. Cal!"

"So what? You know, the thing I can't understand is how you and I, who came from the *same* background, *same* parents, *same* schools . . . how could we turn out so completely opposite to one another? I mean, you seem to be in favour of all the things that I see are destroying our civilization! Socialism, unions—I suppose you support anarchy and drugs?

I laugh.

"Cal," I say, "it's the Maggie Thatchers and Brian Mulroneys of the world who are destroying it."

"I don't know anything about your Mr. Mulroney," he says, "but *Maggie Thatcher* is the *one* person who has put this country back on its feet, man!"

"Tell that to the unemployed in bloody Lancashire!"

"You go tell it to the bloody coal miners' union, and that treasonous bastard Arthur Scargill!"

"What are we doing tomorrow?" I ask.

"Tomorrow," he says brightly, "I thought we might go to Selborne, if you like. It's supposed to be a nice day."

What a relief! These hammer-and-tongs arguments are beginning to exhaust me. At fifteen, I would shout at him, or he at me, and walk away. Then I grew taller than him, and once, in a fight, I actually hurt him. After that, except for rare instances of communication (like the time I went to his room at University to tell him I'd become a Christian, and he invited me in, most gently and full of curiosity) mostly we withdrew from one another.

Selborne! There is one thing we do agree about: nature, to use the old-fashioned word. The beautiful trees and plains and mountains of the Kenya we grew up in now progressively stripped and denuded and drying, the great game animals machine-gunned to extinction; here in Surrey, the precarious greenery of the South Down threatened, he told me during a long walk, by more and more plans for motorways; back home in Canada, the mercury pollution in Howe Sound, at which, when I tell him about it, he shakes his head with an "Oh *God!*" of angry disgust. If there is one cause that just might see us one day together on a picket line, or carrying placards, it is the destruction of the environment. He is infuriated at the extermination of the African elephants, and sent me a newspaper clipping of President Moi's orders to shoot poachers on sight. Now that we have met again and discovered our polar opposition, Selborne is a perfect place for us to take a break: the literary interest for me, the history of science interest for him; and for both of us, a pleasant summer walk in the English countryside. (Driving to Cornwall a few months later in a little rented car, I turn to my friend, the poet Wilma Vance and say, "It really *is* a 'green and pleasant land' isn't it?" She smiles and nods.)

"What about your hayfever, Cal?"

He shakes his head. "If it gets bad, I take an antihistamine."

It's a forty-five minute drive down deliberately-chosen back roads. Calvin acts the guide as he always did when we were children in Africa.

"See there, the rooks are nesting high. Folk wisdom says it means lots of rain coming. I don't know if it's true."

"What's that yellow stuff we saw growing in the fields out west the other day?"

"Oilseed rape."

"Oh, rape. Big crop in the prairie provinces. I was driving through Saskatchewan, and the CBC Radio newsreader said 'Rape is up across the province.' It startled me at first, till I realized what it was."

Wilma Vance would have hooted with laughter at the verbal ambiguity. Calvin makes no response. He will have nothing to do with anything the least bit off-colour. It's not prudishness, however. What is it? Violence, even death may be discussed, but nothing tinged in any way with sex. My father too drew the line at things I found amusing, if there was a hint of smuttiness to them. Some kind of warrior culture? I can't get it.

"For some reason, I always get lost here," Calvin says, with a middle-aged chuckle. "Look at the map will you, and tell me if I turn left or right at this junction."

I study the map and tell him left.

"Yes, yes *of course!*" he says impatiently, as we come to the T. "I've been here dozens of times, I don't know *why* I don't remember it."

As a child he would not have made such a confession to me. The walls of seniority were thicker then, because a three-year age difference at ten or fifteen—or even twenty—is a huge chunk of your life. He would not have wanted then to reveal any weakness or uncertainty. Now, at forty-seven and fifty, we're just about levelled out.

In the churchyard, after we have stood and looked at Gilbert White's grave, Calvin waits patiently as I fiddle with the camera to get a picture of another tombstone. "Hale," it reads, the surname of my neighbour in Vancouver.

"Right," he says, when the shutter clicks, "now we climb the Hanger. You can see the Zigzag there, but I sometimes get lost here too, believe it or not."

"I think I'll leave my camera in the car," I say. "Will it be safe?"

His quick "Yes, yes," makes me suddenly realize that this is one of his established visitor trips. Living so close to

London, Calvin and Mary have many family visitors coming through from Africa, and now me from Canada. I too have my tourist repertoire, ranging from the one-hour trip to Little Mountain to see the flowers and the view, to the day hike up Diamond Head, to the five-day circuit of the Bowron Lakes in rented canoes.

"Have you read Gilbert White's book?" I ask, as we begin climbing on the path.

"*The Natural History of Selborne?* You know, I never have. It's something I've always meant to do, but I never had a copy in my hands at the right time."

"You *must* read it," I say. "Do you know, it's about the most widely reprinted book in English outside of Shakespeare and the Bible."

"Good Lord!"

"The *History* came out seventy years before *Origin of Species,* and White is much more interesting than Darwin."

Calvin climbs in silence. I've said too much. Let him form his own opinion. I make a mental note to look for a really nice copy, and send it to him for Christmas or a birthday. Cal and Mary kept sending presents for years after I ceased responding. Now that I've made contact again, and met the children, I think it would be nice to resume the practice. I'll go up to London, to Foyle's if it's still there, and get a fine old nineteenth-century edition with engravings. He'll love it. Caught up in the excitement of this idea, I start lecturing Cal again:

"White's more important than either Darwin or Linnaeus, in a way. They were organisers of information, systematizers. But White was curious as to the *why* of everything. Why do cats love fish when they *so* detest water? Why is this water rat holed up to hibernate in a potato field miles from the river—is it because of the potatoes, or does he just prefer a change of surroundings for winter? He brought psychology into it, and tried to figure out how animals thought and decided things."

Calvin climbs steadily up the hill. I wonder what he is

thinking. Earlier, Mary showed me a clipping from a magazine: somewhere in the U.S. a veterinary psychologist had
begun a weekly column. One reader wrote to ask how to
alleviate his poodle's distress when he left for work. The
columnist replied: slip away from the apartment in casual
clothes, and change to a suit in the car or at the office.
"Isn't that *ridiculous!*" Mary's nose curled up in amusement.

"There you are," says Calvin brightly. We have come to
the top of the Zigzag. "That's the Wishing Stone," he points.
I go over to it and read the information board. I am glad
that I have not brought my camera. For once, I can really
take my time, and look at things, instead of thinking all the
while about shots.

"Come along, Alistair!"

"Hold on."

Calvin has set off along the Hanger. I remember us bike-
riding as kids. He'd wait for me at the top of the hill, and
when I'd come puffing up, he'd take off again. Now, I
resist his lead. I will finish reading.

He comes back to see what's holding me up.

"That's the Wishing Stone," he calls.

"I know. I'm reading about it."

Patiently, he turns around and studies the grass about
him. Still I'm not done. He comes up to me.

"They carried it here," I say.

"Who did?"

"White and his brothers."

"*Carried* it?"

"Yeah."

"You mean that stone wasn't here originally?"

"No. They brought it over in a cart from Faringdon, and
then carried it up the Zigzag. Three of them."

For a few silent seconds he contemplates this information.

"Good God!" he cries. "What a waste of time!"

I laugh aloud. The dozens of people he must have
brought up here and pointed out the stone to them . . . but

when confronted with the significance of wishing, the practical man in him rebels with derision. The image of three eighteenth-century gentlemen, in their shirtsleeves and their waistcoats, struggling to roll the one-ton piece of rock up to the top of the Hanger, so that people can close their eyes and make wishes, is just too ludicrous for him to take seriously.

"Come on," he says. "Let's go."

The path along the top of the Hanger is very beautiful, running under oaks and other cool, deciduous trees. Calvin keeps up a running commentary on the flora and fauna. Cranesbill at our feet . . . a blue titmouse on a branch.

"Tell me about your job," I ask. He works in vaccine production for a giant drug manufacturer. Wilma Vance, with her poet's instinct for getting to the nub of things, visited him several years ago, and came back and told me my brother was a fanatic, obsessed with the elimination of viruses from the earth—which was news to me.

"I wouldn't know where to begin," he says. "I'd have to fill in so much."

"Just tell me about the latest debate you're involved in at work."

Calvin thinks briefly, then tells me there are two schools of thought about subtyping particularly elusive viruses. If you don't correctly identify the subtype of an outbreak, your vaccine won't work, with tragic results and very angry people. In the older method, you spread out the sample physically in a centrifuge, and then subject it to ultraviolet light, and get a readout on a printer. The newer method uses enzyme replacement. A young scientist in his lab wants to switch wholly to the enzyme method but Calvin is more cautious, and waits for convincing proof.

Immediately, I'm reminded of a scene from my own life: a colleague decided to teach the second-year literature survey course backwards, beginning with T.S. Eliot, and ending with *Beowulf.* The Dean of Canyon College thought this was too unconventional, and might jeopardize our transfer status with the universities. He suggested I write to the universities.

"It's not necessary," I said. "I'm the Department Coordinator, and I've approved her course outline. Period."

"Be reasonable, Alistair!" the Dean said. "Just phone the UBC English Department, and ask if they have any objections. It's the students' transfer credit we're concerned about, not our professional egos."

"And if I have to phone for approval, don't you realize that compromises our independence? We're a College, not a colony!"

To Calvin I say, "Maybe one reason we've grown up to hold such different views of the world, Cal, is simply the experiences we've had."

"What do you mean by that?"

"Your job requires you to be ultra-careful and conservative. Otherwise epidemics break out and vast numbers of people get sick and die. My job as an English professor means that I'm constantly innovating, challenging the status quo and being skeptical."

"So am I," he says. "I can't see the difference you're trying to make out."

Suddenly he points to a line of white flecks in the underbrush. "Look, look!" he says. "Fox's been worrying the rabbits."

Once again, I find myself astonished at his English vocabulary. I couldn't think of uttering a sentence like that. His children call their running shoes trainers, whereas he and I grew up calling them tackies. *Fox's been worrying the rabbits* indeed! In any case, I don't believe it; there's too much of it around. I go over and pick up a bit of the white fluff.

"It's not rabbit fur, Cal. It's paper."

"Is it?" His voice is humble and curious. He comes over and crumbles some of the white pulp between thumb and finger. "Paper," he says, "you're quite right! Fox's been worrying the paper." I turn aside and clear my throat.

At the end of the Hanger we come down into the wire fence of a farmer's cow pasture, and there is no footpath.

"Again!" says Calvin. "How do I manage to *do* it!"

"We're not in any hurry," I say. "We're not going to die of exposure."

"It *irks* me though. The way is clearly marked, and yet I miss it almost every time." He shakes his head in irritated amusement.

Back in the car, our feet soaked and muddy, we begin the drive home in silence. A great outing! For some reason, I suddenly begin explaining to him the politics of Canadian publishing, how we're swamped with foreign books. I explain how, in the lucrative textbook market, it's nothing for an American publisher to ship up ten spare copies of a text they've already published, for consideration in Ontario. Whereas a Canadian publisher would have to spend all the overhead costs of a full print run, just to *get* the ten copies—with no guarantee the book will be adopted, and no possibility of selling it in the States or elsewhere outside Canada. I tell him how publishers are being bought up by heartless conglomerates. Suddenly, I touch a trigger.

"What do you mean 'multi-national corporations'!" he objects loudly. "You talk as though there aren't *people* involved. If you've got a problem with some publisher in New York, why don't you just sit down and write the guy a letter? They're reasonable beings. They have to live in the world too."

"Come on man, I don't have to reinvent the bloody wheel!" I yell impulsively into the windrush of the car. "Don't tell me the Shell Company, for instance, exists to do good in the world. It exists to make money!"

"I think the Shell Company does one hell of a *lot* of good in the world," he says firmly, sounding just like our father. "For one thing, it employs a good many black people in Africa who would probably starve to death without it. And yet you have all these idiot socialists calling for 'disinvestment.' Wishful-thinking bloody morons!"

Angry at myself for my outburst, I ride along in silence. *We had a good day at Selborne*, I think to myself. *Just let it go.* But Calvin's the one who won't leave it now.

"You know," he says, "I like people to express their opinions. I like them to express them *forcibly*, as you do. But the thing I cannot understand about you armchair socialists is that you speak with such *vehemence* on certain topics, and yet you don't actually *know* anything about what you're talking about."

"That's not true."

"Then tell me, have you ever personally met a board member of a multinational corporation?"

"Not that I can think of."

"And yet you can presume to tell me what goes on in their minds. They're human beings, man."

"But their motive is money. The Foundation you work for is different. The man who started it made a fortune from a medical patent, but he didn't then go and gobble up all the profit-making businesses in the world and change them to leaner, meaner money machines. He and his partner put their profits into scientific research and development, where it ought to be."

"Look there," Cal says, with a sudden lowering of voice, "that's the beginning of the Down. And over there," he points, "is the Pilgrim's Way to Canterbury. We must go there before you leave."

Next morning, I wake to the sound of a motor. My brother is mowing his lawn. On this country property he's just bought, the lawn is bigger than a football field, so he's gotten himself a little red Japanese tractor mower, and, with his earmuffs on, he is cutting the grass in ever-closing circles, now and then driving over to dump clippings at the edge of the field. As I watch, the children come out, Nigel with a plastic garbage bag, and Diana with a huge old reed basket from Kenya, the biggest *kikapu* I've ever seen. They load up the clippings and begin to carry them up to the other side of the house. In the kitchen, I ask Mary what they're doing. She hands me my coffee, then leans to look out the window.

"They're putting the mow on the compost," she says.

"Why doesn't—" no! It's none of my business.

"What?" says Mary with a pleasant smile.

"Why doesn't Calvin start another compost heap down by the field? Then the kids wouldn't have to carry the clippings. Abolition of slavery!"

She thinks for a moment.

"But when that compost was rotted and ready to put on the flowerbeds, we'd have to carry *it* to where the flowers are. More work in the long run. Easier to carry the mow, you see."

"I didn't think of that."

"What a lovely ring!" says Mary. "Is it your wedding ring?"

"Yes." I take off the heavy gold ring with the tiger's eye, and give it to her to look at. "We weren't going to have them—or Laura was, I wasn't. Too many marriages. Bad luck, I thought. And then, the afternoon before the ceremony, we were getting the house ready, and Laura suddenly said, 'Don't you want a ring?' and I thought, 'Yes, I want one too.' We dashed out before the stores closed, and bought it at an East Indian jewellers just round the corner—a guy from Tanzania. It cost a fortune, but we were strapped for time, and money didn't seem real that day anyway."

"I like it," says Mary, in her soft, upbeat voice. I have noticed how Cal has acquired some of her speech mannerisms, including this upbeat—or perhaps they have developed them together. "Well done," they will say brightly at any slight accomplishment, such as one of the kids writing a letter to a relative.

Mary returns my ring, and I put on a T-shirt and shorts, and go out to help the kids move the clippings. With bare hands, I pile the wet grass into a garbage bag, and lug it round the house to the compost. Diana and Nigel and I are an assembly line, moving the mow, smiling when we cross paths, saying little. When the job is finished, Calvin pours me a beer, and we sit on the crazy paving round the pool.

"God, you were lucky to get this place!" I say impulsively.

"Hm." Calvin nods. "Did you *read* that book I sent you, *The Kenyatta Succession?*" he asks.

"Yeah, yeah. What a tale! All that political manoeuvring before the Old Man's death. But what interested me most was all the Shakespearean language. I taught one of the authors, you know. I taught him Shakespeare."

"'Anti-Stock-Theft-Squad'!" says Cal in disgust. Then he launches into tales about how bad things are in Africa. He's outraged at the breakdown in public values, the corruption and inefficiency in the civil service. Insistently he repeats stories he told me three days ago about Mama Ngina and the Kenyatta "family," how they ripped the country off. I listen, mildly interested, mildly skeptical. All of a sudden he turns to Paraguay.

"I liked what I saw there," he says. "That's what you call a benevolent dictatorship. They get on with the job, and they don't allow dissent. It's all up front. If someone doesn't like it, fine, they can go somewhere else where there are 'human rights' or something."

No, no, I'm not letting him get away with that. Despite the mellowing effects of the beer, I stop him and dig in for a fight:

"Calvin! How many people have that option, that mobility?"

"Oh *come on*! In South America, people constantly move around from country to country."

"Oh hell!"

"What?"

"My ring!"

"What ring?"

"I've lost my ring."

"You'll find it. It's probably beside your bed, or in the bathroom."

He begins telling me how the East African countries could be the breadbasket of Africa, if only one could get rid of corruption and inefficiency. I sense that deep down he is grieving because we have lost our place in Africa. I thought about my children's future, and decided to emigrate to Canada. Calvin's job was Africanized for political expediency, and after some travels around the world he was quietly moved to the home base in England. His passport is British. Part of him would like to go "home" to Nairobi; part of him is at home here in the English countryside, giving a smile and a thumbs-up to his neighbours as he passes them getting into their cars. No big deal for us— not the diaspora of the Jews, or tribulations of the Vietnamese boat people. But a sense of loss all the same. Calvin rambles on in disgust about the *Wa-Benzi*—that "tribe" defined by their ownership of expensive cars which are the fruit of bribery and graft.

Suddenly a different thought strikes me: Calvin's disgust at the breakdown of the infrastructure in the ex-colonies comes not only from his personal sense of loss. He gets outraged whenever systems break down from weakness or neglect. Order is a priority with him. His task is to order things in the world, and make them run smoothly. In his job, he's a techno-warrior fighting against disease with the latest proven methods. He's Carl Jung's *logos* rampant, "the abstracting and dividing intelligence," which brings order upon chaos by the strength of will. He is the older brother.

In me, the emphasis is more towards *eros*, "the function of relationship," the female principle. Connection rather than control. Is it as simple as that? By nurture or by nature we operate out of different hemispheres of the brain.

Some motive prompts me to tell Cal a story about my son Colin:

"One night," I say, "when he was fifteen, he came home and left me a message on the kitchen table. I came in at midnight from my class in Sechelt, exhausted from the long day, the ferry ride there and back, and here was Colin soliciting my wisdom: He'd been advised he must take Math 10 and Science 10 in summer school, or else repeat Grade 10. He wrote to me, 'Wouldn't it be easier to just go on to Grade 11, and repeat Math 10 and Science 10 in the course of the year?' I wrote him back: 'Colin, as you know, I'm not too familiar with the B.C. school system, so I don't have a real good take on your question. But generally in life I've found that when there are two ways of doing something, the hard way, and the easy way, the hard way is the way to go. It usually is easier in the long run.' And for my birthday, Colin wrote me a story called 'Always The Hard Way, or The Summer We Built The Boat.' He was going to type it up, but a girlfriend offered to do it, so he let her. But on my birthday, he still didn't have it, and he came by the next day with a patched together disaster of a manuscript, half typed, half hand-written, and three spelling errors in the title!"

Calvin is laughing harder than I have seen him laugh since I arrived on this visit.

"What?"

"*You!*" he says, "Complaining about *him*! That's a turn of the tables."

I look at him and wonder what he means.

"You mean—"

"You sound like Father, complaining about *you!*"

I try to remember what he is talking about, but my memory is blank.

"Don't you remember on the Kiambu golf course: 'Alistair! Stop chasing ruddy grasshoppers, and get on with the game!'?"

I hear my father's voice in his. Against my denial, the memories begin to flow in: On the golf course at Kiambu, I have paused to scrape the fresh soil off the top of a mole-hill with my club, and my father is yelling at me. Later, I am nineteen and have succeeded in replacing the gearbox of my Austin with an overhauled one I bought at one of the wrecking shops on River Road; I am in the bathroom, scrubbing grease marks off my arms in triumph, when my father storms in and yells with a savage frown: "Are any of those tools still any *good*, or shall I have them all *thrown out?*"

I stare at him in amazement, then realize what he is talking about. I left some wrenches on the lawn where I had been working on the car, and now it is raining.

"Father," I say, fearful as I speak that he might explode and die, or maybe even hit me for the first time in his life, "they're chrome-vanadium stainless steel you know." He turns and walks away quaking, muttering as he goes: "Don't you be disrespectful to me, young man." And now, three decades later, my brother hears me storming on about my own careless son, and he laughs his head off.

That night at supper, I announce: "I really have lost my ring."

"It'll turn up," says Calvin. "Is it valuable?"

"It's his *wedding* ring," says Mary. "Where do you think you might have lost it?"

"I've come to the conclusion it must be in the compost," I say. "You see, when we were gathering the grass clippings for the compost, my fingers got wet and probably shrunk a bit, and the ring slipped off. Do you have such a thing as yellow pages?"

"In the phone book, you mean?"

Calvin leaves to watch the TV news. Mary opens a drawer and hands me the small directory. The yellow pages section is so short that I am not hopeful, but sure enough there it is under "Tools for Hire." Not one, but two places in town that rent metal detectors. Oh, this is going to be fun! I am ninety-nine percent sure the ring is in that pile of grass clippings—where else could it be? I'll probably have to rent the machine for four hours minimum, if not a whole day. We'll find the ring in five minutes, and then we can all go out back in the hayfield, and see what we can find.

Roman coins! Tracer bullets from World War II dogfights. Something valuable maybe, or else just old rusty nails. I've never used a metal detector before. I can't wait to put the headphones on and listen for that geiger crackle. The kids will love it.

I go to join Calvin at the TV.

"You want to watch any more?" he asks, when his programme ends.

"No," I say. "I want a belt of scotch, if that's all right."

"Help yourself." He switches off the set, and I head to the liquor cabinet.

Most days, Cal will drink one beer before supper. Mary very occasionally takes a glass of wine. That's it. Compared to them, I and most of my friends in Canada must seem like raging alcoholics. The litre of duty-free scotch that I brought them has gone, and I bought another litre, and it's half gone, and I am the only one who's touched it. I sit back down with the ice cubes clinking in my full glass. I resist feeling embarrassed.

"I'm going to rent a metal detector tomorrow, Cal."

"Oh." He looks at me, uncomprehending.

"My ring must be in the compost. Those things have a range of six inches. I can run it through the pile of clippings in no time at all."

His face breaks into laughter. "No, no, no!" he laughs. "A metal detector!" He makes it sound utterly ridiculous—as ridiculous as pouring maple syrup over bacon and pancakes. (I think back to the first Canadians I ever met, two nurses on the S.S. *Kenya Castle* in 1960, and how I thought *them* outlandish for pouring syrup onto bacon. I recall my old Scottish friend's story about lining up for Thanksgiving Dinner on an American ship in WWII, and seeing the cranberry sauce: "Hey Mac, wi' ya look a' this? The bloody Yanks are puttin' jam on their meat!") I don't respond to Cal. He can laugh if he likes, I am going to rent it. Damn! It occurs to me that I'll have to borrow his car to get to town. Well, I will walk if necessary. I am very determined.

As I go off to bed, I recall how the last time I was in town, I asked a man how to get to the train station.

"*Train* station?" he said, in apparent bewilderment. "The *train* station? Do you mean you want the *railway* station?"

"It's the *train* I'm interested in, more than the rails," I answered in a rude flash; but I smiled, and he gave me the directions.

Now I crawl into bed, my mind quite firm about renting that machine.

In the morning, at the breakfast table, Cal says: "I've been thinking about your ring problem, Alistair, and I've come up with a solution."

I have the solution already! I think, but hold back from speaking.

"I've got this old torn sheet," he says. "We'll just sift through the compost with that. Should find it okay."

I take a breath. *All right,* I think. *We'll do that if you want. We'll do that for precisely TEN minutes! And then I'm going to the Tool Hire place.*

We stand holding the sheet folded in half over one corner of the large compost heap. Cal has thrown a few handfuls of clippings into the fold, and now we slowly saw the four corners of the sheet up and down, and watch the little trickle of green grass falling out of the tear. The heap of clippings covers an area the size of a room. I look at my watch. *Fifteen minutes,* I think. *I'll take fifteen minutes of this nonsense!*

"No, stand on this side," Cal says. . . . "Okay, look, you just hold it still and I'll move my side."

It goes on like that for half an hour. We have searched through one tenth of the pile of clippings.

You are forty-seven years old! I tell myself. *Put down the damn sheet and walk away, and go rent a metal detector!*

I look at my watch. *All right,* I think, *one hour. Just for harmony.* And having made that decision, I feel patient and easy again. One full hour, and I will put it down. I think of Ghandi, passive resistance. I watch the minute hand

patiently. I reach in to break up a little clog of green clippings. My fingers touch cold, hard gold.

"Here it is!"

"Well done," says Calvin. He shakes and folds the sheet,
and walks ahead of me to the kitchen. "He found it," he
says.

"Well done," says Mary.

"Thanks a lot, man," I say.

"Oh . . ." he dismisses it with a grin. But I picture him
now sometimes, when friends are over, telling about his
brother the absurd North American, in sentences broken up
with laughter: "So he says he's going to go and rent a
bloody *metal detector!*"

"What did you do?" someone asks.

I imagine Cal turning to him, and swallowing, and his
laughter subsiding into a deadpan look. "We took a sheet
and sifted through and found the ring," he says offhanded-
ly. "Metal detector!" he wrings one last echo of a laugh out
of it.

Here, in Vancouver, I've just re-read *The Natural History
of Selborne.* Poor Gilbert White! So riled about the
swallows:

> March 9, 1772
> Dear Sir,
> As a gentleman and myself were walking on
> the fourth of last November round the
> sea-banks at Newhaven, near the mouth of the
> Lewes river, in pursuit of natural knowledge,
> we were surprised to see three house-swallows
> gliding very swiftly by us. That morning was
> rather chilly, with the wind at northwest; but
> the tenor of the weather for some time before
> had been delicate, and the noons remarkably
> warm. From this incident, and from repeated
> accounts which I meet with, I am more and
> more induced to believe that many of the

swallow kind do not depart from this island;
but lay themselves up in holes and caverns;
and do, insect-like and bat-like, come forth
at mild times, and then retire again to their
latebrae. Nor make I the least doubt but
that, if I lived at Newhaven, Seaford,
Brighthelmstone, or any of those towns near
the chalk cliffs of the Sussex coast, by
proper observations I should see swallows
stirring at periods of the winter when the
noons are soft. . . .

Listen to him! "More and more induced to believe . . .
nor make I the least doubt . . . by proper observations."
How transparent and childlike is the man's wish to believe
that the swallows are faithful after all. That they *don't*
betray him and all England by going to winter in foreign
lands. *Maybe the swallows hole up under water!* Gilbert
rashly speculates. He studies the swifts, and the house mar-
tins, and the swallows, comparing their dates, trying to
determine which species is the most loyal. What unexpected metaphors we choose on which to let our identities ride,
what stubbornness: "Fox's been worrying the paper." "I'm
going to rent a metal detector." "Do you mean you want
the *railway* station?" "The bloody Yanks are puttin' jam on
their meat!"

One last week I spend at my brother's house, and after
this long vacuum of time, the intensity has exhausted me.
Late at night, I take half a tumbler of scotch and my pipe
and tobacco out by the pool, and sit wondering what's
going on back home. What is Laura doing, and the kids?
Lots of questions. If I needed the answers, I'd phone. They
can wait.

Next morning, I take the train up to London. Charing
Cross Road is cluttered with renovation fences, and
Foyle's Bookshop is unrecognizable—I can't even find the
second-hand section. I feel lost, but am in no mood to ask

for directions. Then, suddenly, I see a familiar up-and-down stripe of books in a wire rack. Coming closer, I realize that the display is of a book I first published at my little press in Vancouver. Son of a gun! He's made it to London. Good for you, buddy. He'll get the Booker Prize. He deserves it. Overflowing with heart, I go up to a Foyle's clerk and he tells me where to find a second-hand *Natural History*.

That evening, after supper, I give Calvin the book, and watch his excited response. He turns carefully from engraving to engraving, sometimes pausing to read a little text. He holds the book like a precious object in his open hands.

"Cal, what got you interested in natural history in the first place?" I ask.

"Well, Ma and Pa bought me a microscope for my tenth birthday, remember?"

"Yes, but they wouldn't just pick a microscope out of the blue."

"No," he agrees. "You're right, they wouldn't."

He stares off into the distance of the English summer sky.

HOW I BECAME A CANADIAN

When I first came to Canada in the sixties, I was already aware of certain legal subtleties of citizenship. I had the experience of coming from the Third World, and had already possessed two different citizenships. When Kenya became independent, and I was selected for a scholarship to Canada, despite being white, by a committee of various races, and from among applicants who were mostly black, I became very emotional: This *is* a democratic country, I said with enthusiasm. *"Harambee!"* ("let's all pull together!"—it was the national motto). Proudly, I went down to register as a Citizen of Kenya.

The clerk took my forms, and studied them. Eventually, he said, "This is not possible now for you to register as citizen of Kenya."

I drew myself erect. "Why not?" I said. "I was born in Kenya. I have lived here most of my life. I am a *mwalimu* at the High School in Kikuyu. I wish to register as a citizen."

"There is a problem that you have already been registered as a citizen of the United Kingdom and Colonies."

"and Colonies'!" said I. He knew the implications of that. I knew them. It was the code phrase to tell British Immigration officers that you were a foreigner, not a resident. *"Nimesaliwa inchi hii, bwana!* I was born in this country."

"There's just a problem, you see, that you have been registered as citizen of U.K. and Colonies, and this must be *renounced* first."

"Oh, I see. Of course I'll renounce it. What do you have, a bible?"

"Well, you have to see the British High Commissioner, and then bring us the Certificate of Renunciation."

"I see." That didn't sound so good.

I walked directly to the British High Commission, before I could think too much.

"Good morning, sir. May I help you?"

"Yes," I said brightly. "I'd like to . . . renounce my British Citizenship."

As I spoke the words, they fell on my ears like a doom. I flashed ahead, paranoid, and saw myself languishing in some rancid jail in Buenos Aires or Katmandu—with no help from the British Consul. I flashed back to all those times when I had come close to royalty: the Queen at Government House in 1953 when her father died while she was visiting Kenya, and I saw her as Queen before the English did; the church in Bulawayo, where I sat directly behind the Queen and Prince Philip, so that they'd have heard my faintest cough; the cattle judging at the Kenya Agricultural Society's annual Royal Show in 1959, when I sat on the bleachers behind Princess Margaret, and heard the angry exchange among aides de camp about whether or not Her Highness should travel in a Land-Rover, and finally, the military commander turning and saying "Take the bloody thing away!" All these privileged moments of Britishness were about to fall away: the Union Jack would be no longer my flag, but in its place that violent green and red and black tricolour ("with the white lines in between, holding the country together" as some of my friends used to say) with the primitive shield in front, and the crossed Maasai spears. All of this was roiling around in my gut, as I waited for the efficient secretary to return to the counter. Bailing out. Was I doing that? Marooning myself, and Julia, and the kids?

"If you'll just take a seat over there," the efficient secretary pointed, "and fill out this form." She smiled, making my treachery seem ambivalent at worst. I filled it out, and took it back to her.

"Thank you, sir. That'll be ten shillings please, and I'll have your certificate ready in a few minutes."

I would be stretching the truth, if I said that the scales fell from my eyes at that precise moment. The British are a nation of shopkeepers, yes, the government itself in business to grab a tax on everything *including* renunciation of citizenship. Here I had been innocently worrying about what this British secretary thought of me jumping ship, and all she was thinking of was the ten shillings she had to reap from my desertion.

Having presented my certificate of renunciation, I was duly registered as a Kenya Citizen.

On my first night in the student married housing apartment in Vancouver—Julia and the kids were in Montreal, spending a week with her sister—I turned on the second-hand TV I'd bought. Lester Pearson's face came on the screen. Underneath, a white-on-black caption read, "The Prime Minister."

"God damn it! What kind of a country is this?" I railed. Back in Kenya, a few weeks before, I had been lying on my stomach one night, watching *Bonanza* on the newly available TV, when suddenly the picture disappeared, and the national shield and spears appeared, and a familiar accelerating drumbeat commenced the national anthem. Then Jomo Kenyatta appeared live, to announce the deportation of some offensive whites.

"MY GOVERNMENT WILL NOT TOLERATE . . ." Jomo

began. Good God! Imagine Canada—a country where they had to put a caption underneath, to remind people who the head of the government is!

In those first years in Canada, I yearned to belong, and was ever critical of the sloppiness around me. "When're those people in Africa gonna come to their senses," my neighbour said over the fence in Kitsilano, where we'd moved from student housing. "When're you going to get yourself educated?" I felt like replying.

Then Julia and I split up. She went back to Africa with the kids. I stayed on, finishing another degree. My "cousin" Pete Johnson in Kenya wrote to say: "It seems to me, when a man's made his bed, he ought to lie in it." I froze off my African connections.

Bitterness. Divorce. Oh shit! I came to think that I should stay in Canada, become a Canadian. I made up my mind and married again, a Canadian. We went off to New York State on a teaching exchange. We came back, and that broke up. One day, I marched into the Citizenship Branch and asked how I could become a Canadian Citizen.

"You have to have resided here for five years," the clerk told me.

"I've resided here for nine," I said.

"Then, there's no problem. We need three referees."

But there was a problem. My nine years translated down to four, because my arrival in September was ignored—they only counted calendar years from January 1. And the student years were counted as half, and the year on exchange didn't count at all.

I objected to this last. "Listen, I was *employed* in Canada. My *paycheque* was deposited at the Bank of Montreal in Park Royal. I paid income tax in Canada, that year."

"Well, for tax purposes, you *were* a Canadian resident, true," the clerk said. "But for citizenship, you were out of the country."

"Thanks a lot!"

A year and a bit later, I went down, quite shaky, because

by now my student visa was long expired, and I had been able to work only by virtue of a Social Insurance card that I'd obtained as a graduate teaching assistant at UBC. In other words, I'd been illegal for a couple of years, and every time I saw a police cruiser inching along Panorama Drive, where I lived, I'd felt very stressed. I had a girlfriend who taught me to ski, and she said we should really go to Mount Baker, where most of the runs were junior and inter-mediate, and when I said no, I couldn't cross the border, she said, "Oh, you're *soo* uptight!" And then, a Calgary lawyer from Indonesia went down to Seattle, where his sick mother's plane had been diverted because of poor weather in Vancouver, and when he tried to cross back into Canada at Blaine, they held him up while they checked on the computer, and deported him and his sick parent on the next plane back to Indonesia. At any rate, I went down and presented myself a second time to Immigration at the foot of Burrard.

The officer perused my file, and asked: "You work at Canyon College?"

"Yes."

"The English Department?"

"Yes."

"My son tried to get in there. He was failed on the entrance exam."

"No, there's no failing. It's a placement test. Perhaps he got placed in the College Preparatory course."

"My son remedial!" the man snorted. "All these foreigners pouring into the country, and my son has to drive all the way from West Vancouver to Douglas College, because you people failed him!"

I decided I had better just shut up and wait. I said no-thing, and after a few more minutes of delay, I was finally given clearance to be a citizen.

Phew! A Canadian citizen.

But was I? Again and again people heard my accent and asked if I was English. Australian? "No," I said, "I came from Kenya, but I'm a Canadian now."

What the hell did they want? Hadn't I founded a small Canadian press, and fought off the foreigners who dump their cultural remainders on us? As a college English teacher hadn't I challenged people to stop putting only dead British and American writers on their reading lists like they did at UBC—instead, hadn't I shown the way by having my students read Ondaatje, Laurence, Munro, Thomas, Wiebe, Roch Carrier, Herschell Hardin, Atwood and dozens of other living Canadians? At a time when there were few qualified Canadians applying for teaching jobs, hadn't I fought the Dean to hire a Canadian, even though she was only twenty-two with no teaching experience? I even revised the application form for employees of the College, adding a line that asked: "What is your immigration status in Canada?" And still that irritating question: "Are you from England?" "Are you an Australian?"

The Japanese immigrants have understood the problem, and given it a cultural form, by naming the generations. The *Issei* still live in the old country in their minds, the *Nisei* partly here and partly there, the *Sansei* are bred and born Canadian, even if they did grow up in evacuation camps in their own hostile mother land of Canada, and the *Yonsei*—why the *Yonsei* are so acclimatized, that the term only exists on paper: I've never heard anybody use it.

For us Kenyan-Canadians, it is not so traumatic. We have the same colonial past as the rest of Canada. In many ways, it's easier to come to Canada from Kenya or Trinidad or Pakistan, than it is from the States. Yet it took a long time before I felt I had become a Canadian. I remember exactly how it happened. In 1974, shortly after I became a citizen, I bought a new car, a Fiat 124—well, not exactly brand new; it was a demonstrator. Price reduced from $4,200 to $3,900. It had 3,000 kilometres on the clock. Fair enough. And six years later, the windshield-wiper motor quit one day. I investigated, and found the brushes were gone, a pair of little carbon brushes, half a centimetre long. I went down to the Fiat agent, Pacific InterAuto, and asked the price of a new windshield-wiper motor. $180! And the brushes couldn't be worth more than a buck or two—probably eighty-five cents. A hundred and eighty bucks? My dander rose. And suddenly I was in Kenya: years ago, on my drive to South Africa, my Austin A40 had cracked the front member of the chassis, both sides, and I had had it welded up; after that trip the front wheels remained splayed out a little.

"It looks to me as though the camber angle needs adjusting," my father said grumpily, and walked away. He, who had taught me all kinds of intricate procedures for fixing cars, was too old now to bother with them.

I studied the workshop manual. In the Specifications section it gave a camber angle, two degrees, but there was nothing at all about adjustment, no diagram anywhere. I went down to the Overseas Motor Corporation, the Austin agent.

"Nineteen forty-eight A40," I said. "Is there a camber adjuster?"

"This is Parts, sir. Service department is round the side."

"No. I do my own. I just want you to look in the book and tell me if it shows a camber adjuster?"

The little black-haired Brit studied the parts book for a while, and then said: "It appears that the A40 camber angle is not adjustable."

"I don't believe it!" I said. "Do you mean to tell me that if you have a car come in here with a cracked chassis, you tow it away to the wrecking yard? Come on! What *do* you do to adjust the camber angle?"

The Brit glared at me, then half turned his head and called over his shoulder: "Patel! Could you come and look at this a moment please?"

A young East Indian man came from the parts shelves to the counter, and studied me, the book, and his white fellow worker.

"What do we do, for camber on an A40?" the parts man asked.

"Those are wishbone shocks," Patel said. "If they need adjustment, we send it to B and G out on Enterprise Road by Timsales, and they heat the upper arm and straighten."

So I drove to Timsales, found B & G, and had them take care of my upper wishbone arms. It cost sixteen shillings.

But this was Canada. A hundred and eighty bucks for a wiper motor.

"Don't you stock brushes for the wiper motor?" I asked.

"For a Fiat? No sir! Sorry, we don't carry those sorts of parts at all."

"Come on!" I wanted to say. "What do *you* do when a Fiat's wiper motor brushes wear out? Don't tell me you replace the whole unit, at a cost of $180—that's five percent of what I paid for the car!"

Something in me vetoed this approach. And that is the moment when I began to become a Canadian.

"Is that right?" I said.

I backed off from the counter, lost in my own thoughts.

"No, I'm sorry, sir. We don't carry small items like that. Why . . . what is the problem?"

"Well, Jeez, all I need is the brushes, you know. Fifty cents or something. And a replacement motor is a hundred and eighty bucks."

"Yeah, right." The parts manager at Pacific InterAuto is on my side. "Patel!" he calls over his shoulder, "Where can this gentleman get windshield wiper motor brushes?"

From the parts shelves, a middle-aged East Indian man emerges.

"Windshield wiper motor brushes?" he says, his double-u's almost v's.

"Yeah, just the brushes." (*Is* it the same man who helped me in Nairobi twenty-five years ago?)

"There's a place called Western Starter, up on Victoria around 36th Avenue. Try there."

Western Starter says no. I stand around, looking bereft, till someone asks, "What's the problem?"

"All I need is carbon brushes, you know? A buck or two.

To replace the wiper motor is two hundred!"

"Yeah, yeah, I understand. Why don't you try, um, Barratt Autoelectric, at Twelfth and Arbutus. They might be able to help you."

The parts man at Barratt takes the stub of my wornout brush and examines it. "Could be about the same as a '57 Chevy," he says. He goes behind and brings some brushes, and we study them together. The brushes seem exactly the same, or perhaps a trifle too wide.

"Well if they're not dead on, I can file them a bit, right?" I say.

"Oh yah."

Eighty-five cents a pair. I buy two pairs.

Moving out of there to my Fiat, I think, "Wow! You finally became a Canadian!"

And the windshield wiper worked.

That's the end of the story, except to confess that I couldn't resist going back to Pacific InterAuto, and found out that Mr. Patel was indeed from Kenya, though he wasn't the one who worked at OMC. It's a fairly common name.

"So, how long you have been here?" he asked.

"Since sixty-four."

"I came in seventy-two."

"Sasa tunakua waCanada!" Now we're Canadians!

"Kweli! Asante sana!" Right! Many thanks!

That pleasant Swahili custom: when you have a conversation with someone, at the end they thank you. *Asante sana!*

I shook hands with Mr. Patel, and walked out of there whistling.

Power for a fine flexible performance comes from a four-
cylinder valve-in-head engine
of compact design. It is of
73·17 cu. in. capacity developing
42 horse-power at 4,500 r.p.m.